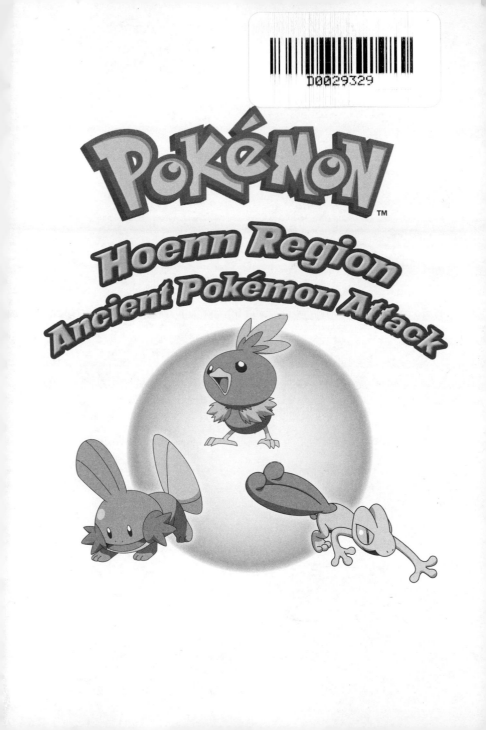

# POKÉMON™

## Hoenn Region
## Ancient Pokémon Attack

# POKÉMON ™

## Sinnoh Region
## The Power of Three

Adapted by Helena Mayer

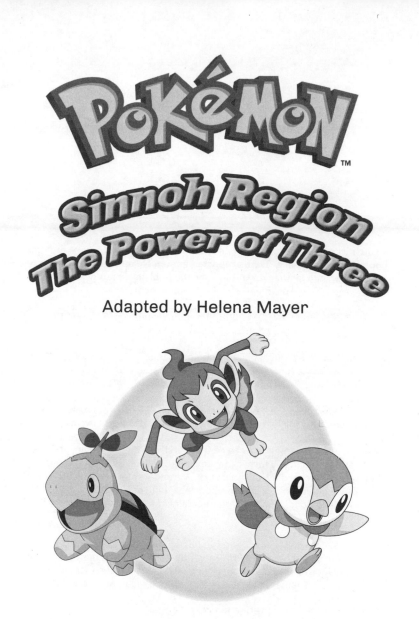

Scholastic Inc.

This book is a work of fiction. Names, characters, places, and incidents are either the product of the author's imagination or are used fictitiously, and any resemblance to actual persons, living or dead, business establishments, events, or locales is entirely coincidental.

ISBN 978-1-338-74655-6

10 9 8 7 6 5 4 3 2 1          21 22 23 24 25

Printed in China          62
First printing 2021

# CHAPTER 1

**D**eep in the Sinnoh region, a man ran through an abandoned factory, dodging energy blasts. A flock of Golbat were on his tail. The man ducked and weaved. He darted left. He zoomed right. But the Golbat would not give up.

A lightning bolt seared through the air. Direct hit! The man screamed and fell to the ground. Everything went dark.

When he opened his eyes, a woman with purple hair loomed over him. She wore a Team Galactic jumpsuit and an evil smile. It was Jupiter, one of the most powerful and dangerous members of the criminal organization known as Team Galactic. A snarling Skuntank stood by her side.

"I see we've finally caught up to you," Jupiter said. "Now — show your face!"

The man ripped off his disguise and revealed his true identity. It was Looker, the International Police officer! He had come all this way to catch Team Galactic. But they'd caught him instead.

"The jig is up," he admitted. He stood up and dusted off his brown detective coat.

"That coat is *so* out of style," Jupiter cracked.

Looker just grinned. "I think you should know, for a lady you're quite rude."

She scowled. "Isn't that a shame? However, there are many things I'm dying to ask you about. For starters, how much do you know about *us*?"

Skuntank's claws began to glow — a sure sign that a Slash attack was on its way. Looker didn't want to answer any of Jupiter's questions. But it was starting to look like he wouldn't have much choice. . . .

Not far away, Ash, Brock, and Dawn had no idea that one of their friends was in trouble. They were relaxing in Floaroma Town, watching TV.

"For this year's Pokémon contest there's a brand-new schedule on tap," the TV announcer reported. "To the east of Mt. Coronet, in Daybreak City, it's the exciting Daybreak Contest! And, for the first time in quite a while, it will be a Double Performance!"

"Double Performance, wow!" Dawn exclaimed.

Brock checked his Pokégear. "Daybreak City's right on the way to Sunyshore City," he said.

"What're you gonna do, Dawn?" Ash asked.

"Enter the Daybreak Contest, of course!" Her proud Water-type Pokémon, Piplup, flapped its wings and chattered in excitement.

"So you're gonna give that Double Performance a shot," Ash said.

"Right!" Dawn cheered. "Truth is, I've really been dying to try a Double Performance one more time. It's important, since I didn't win before; know what I mean?"

"You *bet* I do!" Ash said. "Great!"

His little yellow Electric-type Pokémon, Pikachu, thought it was great, too.

They set out right away. As they walked through the flowered meadows of Sinnoh, everyone was excited. Pikachu and Piplup led the way, singing. It seemed like nothing could go wrong.

Until something did.

Pikachu spotted something in the meadow and stopped in its tracks. Piplup stopped singing.

"Piplup?" it questioned.

Ash looked at his Pokémon in concern. "What's up?"

Pikachu didn't answer. It ran into the flowers. That's when Ash realized what Pikachu had seen. There was a wounded Pokémon in the meadow.

"Pikachu, wait!" Ash cried. He and his friends followed Pikachu to the injured Pokémon.

"A Meowth," Ash said, upset by how pale and still the Pokémon looked. Its eyes were closed. Pikachu gave it a gentle shake, but it didn't stir.

"It looks bad," Dawn said in a worried voice.

Suddenly, Meowth gave a mighty shudder. It was awake! It stumbled to its feet, rubbing its head. Then it opened its eyes — and screamed.

"Yipes!" Meowth shouted. "It's the *twerps*!"

Ash couldn't believe his ears. "It's Team Rocket's Meowth," he cried.

"Two points," Meowth said, sounding annoyed. Then terror passed over his face. "What about Jessie and James?"

Before he could find an answer, Meowth collapsed to the ground.

Ash hurried to help him. Meowth wasn't exactly a *friend*, but Ash couldn't stand to see any Pokémon in pain. Even this one. "Meowth, you okay?"

Brock carefully lifted Meowth. "Meowth needs medical help," he said. "We'll talk later."

Fortunately, Brock knew exactly what to do. He always carried his Pokémon healing equipment with him. He applied a healing spray to Meowth's wounds.

"Man, that spritz kinda stings," Meowth complained weakly.

"Now I just need to put a wrapping on it," Brock said. He wound a bandage around Meowth's injured arm.

Once Meowth was taken care of, Ash couldn't wait to get some answers. "What happened to you?"

Just the thought of it made Meowth fume. "It was those fashion freaks!" he shouted.

Uh-oh. Ash and his friends knew exactly what that meant: Team Galactic. What were they up to now?

"**S**ee, we were tailing you twerps, doing that thing we do so well," Meowth explained. "Then, as we were dragging our empty tummies through the forest foraging for food . . ."

Ash, Brock, and Dawn listened carefully as Meowth told his story. He explained that Team Rocket had been wandering in the forest. They had completely lost their way.

There was no food, and there was no way out of the forest. But there *was* a sound like thunder rumbling over their heads. But it wasn't thunder. It was a large, gray airship hovering in the sky. A giant, golden *G* was painted across the steel hull.

Jessie had pointed at the ship. "That mark!"

James recognized it, too. "Freaks of fashion!"

"Yeah, Team Galactic!" Meowth shouted.

"So let's go," Jessie suggested.

"Ho!" James and Meowth agreed.

The ship rocketed through the sky. Team Rocket raced through the forest, trying to keep it in sight. Soon, they reached a large, abandoned factory. They hid behind the bushes and watched as the ship landed in a clearing.

"Heads up, folks," Meowth said. "I think we're gawking at Team Galactic's base!"

Team Rocket decided to take a closer look. They found a ladder and propped it against the side of the factory. Soon they were on the roof. Now all they needed was a way inside.

Finally, Team Rocket found an opening in the roof. It let them peer down into the factory. That's when they spotted Looker, running from Jupiter.

They saw Jupiter's Golbat catch Looker and knock him to the ground.

They saw Jupiter getting ready to attack.

And they saw what they had to do next.

"We've gotta save him, dig?" Meowth said.

James wasn't so sure. "A member of the International Police? Please." Looker was one of the good guys. And Team Rocket *hated* good guys.

"By law, Team Rocket doesn't save the law," Jessie reminded Meowth.

The Pokémon explained his idea. "But doing the right thing for a change might help us put Team Galactic on the fashion garbage heap where those freaks belong!"

James finally got it. "We'd be putting the International Police to work for *us*!"

"Using the good guys to accomplish our evil deeds surely works for me," Jessie agreed.

They chanted together: "Team Rocket's gonna grow and thrive! Those fashion freaks will take a dive! *No jive!*"

Down below, Jupiter's Skuntank was about to attack Looker. But before it could unleash its Slash attack, green vines shot through the air and wrapped around its paw. Skuntank was trapped!

"What the . . . ?" Jupiter looked up.

Team Rocket waved down at her. James's Carnivine had unleashed the Vine Whip attack that left Skuntank all tied up.

"There's room for *one* evil team in this town!" Jessie called down.

"And Team Rocket is its name!" James added.

"Rest easy, police dude," Meowth told Looker. "We're here to save you!"

Looker didn't look particularly pleased. "Not *you* three," he muttered.

Jupiter wasn't any happier to see them. "Incompetent pests," she said. "Stay out of my business!" Then she signaled with a fist in the air.

A moment later, the sky filled with Golbat. They swooped. They swarmed. Their fangs gleamed as they unleashed a powerful attack.

Team Rocket tried to fight back, but it was no use. The powerful, high-pitched sound waves were coming fast and furious. The Golbat worked together, combining their attacks into one enormous explosion. Team Rocket went flying through the air.

And that was the last thing Meowth remembered.

# CHAPTER 4

"Team Galactic may be weird, but they sure pack a wallop!" Meowth told Ash and his friends. "Yup, so we fought the good fight all right. They got their filthy mitts on Jessie and James, but the explosion sent *me* into a solo blastoff. When I came to, I was actually being rescued by you twerps!"

Brock felt bad for the Pokémon. "You've had quite a tough time!"

"Thanks for the save, twerp," Meowth said. Then he jumped to his feet. There was no time to waste. Meowth stomped into the meadow.

"Meowth, hold on!" Ash called, chasing after him.

"Where are you going?" Dawn added.

Meowth turned back, a fierce look on his face. "Jessie and James are waiting for me. Back *there*."

He pointed in the direction he had come from.

Dawn understood. She just couldn't believe it. "You're going back to Team Galactic's base?"

"You could really get hurt!" cried Brock.

Meowth didn't care. He had to save his friends. And he wasn't going to let anyone stop him.

"Okay!" Ash said, when he saw that Meowth wasn't going to listen. "We're going *with* you."

"Let's make sure we're packed up and ready," Brock suggested.

"Right!" his friends agreed. Brock had put Meowth's description of the factory into his Poké-gear to pinpoint its location, so they knew exactly where to go: the Fuego Ironworks.

Meowth was confused. "I appreciate you lugs patching me up," he said. "But you lugs and I are enemies, dig it? I can't take charity from you."

Dawn knew Meowth didn't think he needed their help. But he was wrong. "Think of it like this," she said. "We're helping Looker for *us*."

"Yeah," Brock said. "Looker is a friend. He's helped us out, and now it's our turn to help him."

"Right, so c'mon!" Ash urged Meowth. "Hurry it up and lead us to their base, okay, Meowth?"

When Meowth didn't move, Ash and his friends started off down the road. They knew the Scratch Cat Pokémon would follow.

And he did.

Team Galactic had tossed Team Rocket and Looker into a jail cell. But Jessie wasn't giving up. "Excuse me!" she shouted. "Anybody home?"

Nobody answered. A lazy Skuntank lay on the floor, glaring at the prisoners.

"E-*nough* with the attitude!" she shouted. "I'm going to pluck the fur off your annoying self, strand by strand! Ready or not —"

"Don't touch!" Looker cried.

Jessie's hands wrapped around the bars. Electricity sizzled through the steel. She dropped to the ground, twitching spastically. "Hi, Mommy," she moaned dramatically. "I'm home."

Outside the cell, Skuntank laughed.

"There are booby traps everywhere," Looker explained. "And since electronic devices won't work, we can't use our Poké Balls. Be careful."

While Jessie got her strength back, James tested out one of his Poké Balls. Looker was right. The Poké Ball didn't work.

"Well, I'll be dipped!" he exclaimed.

Jessie burst into angry tears. "Just great," she told Looker. "*Now* you tell us."

Looker sighed. He felt terrible. "I shouldn't have involved you," he said. "I'm sorry."

James couldn't let him take all the blame. "We involved ourselves, don't you see? Our disdain for Team Galactic brought us here!"

The words "Team Galactic" reminded Jessie how angry she was. She jumped up, clenching her fists. "We'll pound those fashion freaks into a fashion pulp!"

"And since we did manage to barge into their base, all that remains is to defeat their boss," James said.

Looker shook his head. "Their boss isn't here."

James was shocked. "If this isn't headquarters, what *is* it?"

"It appears to be their secret factory," Looker explained.

"A factory for secrets?" Jessie asked. The electric zap had muddled her brain.

"Let me explain," Looker said. "At one point in time, this factory was the largest and most successful manufacturer in the entire Sinnoh region. It was closed down due to excessive pollution, but now Team Galactic has been using it as their secret factory, if you will. Secret in the sense that they're using it to make . . . *something*."

But what?

# CHAPTER 5

Looker was right. Team Galactic was using the factory to make something. Something big.

At the center of the Fuego Ironworks stood a secret laboratory. When Jupiter arrived, the Team Galactic scientist was waiting for her. Charon was smiling.

A thin red chain floated in midair. It whirled in a narrow loop, making the room glow.

"Ah, to look upon the exquisite beauty of the Red Chain," Jupiter said. "It's remarkable we could recreate it from the Veilstone City meteorite!"

"Not recreate it, *resurrect* it," Charon corrected her. "Don't forget that the brilliant genius who should be credited with bringing it back into our world is yours truly, known to you as the humble Charon!" He burst into mad laughter.

Jupiter groaned. "I hate that laugh."

Charon laughed even harder.

"What are your plans for the International Policeman?" Jupiter asked.

"Cyrus has already informed me that he has his own special plans for him. . . ."

Cyrus was the leader of Team Galactic. As Jupiter and Charon plotted in the lab, Cyrus was at the top of Mt. Coronet, putting the finishing touches on his plan. For months now, he'd been collecting — *stealing*, really — powerful objects he needed. The Adamant Orb, the Lustrous Orb — his Team Galactic henchmen had obtained them for him. He was finally about to put them to use.

One of his most trusted henchmen, Saturn, was there to help. While Cyrus sat, comfortable inside Team Galactic's secret base, Saturn tried to smash a hole in the side of the mountain.

"Toxicroak, use Rock Smash!" Saturn ordered. The Poison-and-Fighting-type Pokémon aimed a Rock Smash attack at the mountain. The wall of rock exploded, revealing a giant stone gateway. Saturn gasped. The massive door was engraved with strange, elaborate patterns. A golden globe glowed at its center.

Cyrus watched it all on his monitor. He smiled.

Saturn opened up a silver briefcase. A golden lattice emerged and floated toward the stone gateway. When it touched the stone, the gateway crackled with energy.

"Master Cyrus!" Saturn said, excited. "We have found it. This is truly the gateway to Spear Pillar!"

"Yes, very well," Cyrus said. "Block off the area."

"Yes, sir!" Saturn said.

Cyrus was growing impatient. His triumph was so close. But if he rushed, he might get sloppy. "We will not proceed there until all preparations have been made."

*Nothing can stop us now*, Cyrus thought.

Maybe so. But Ash, Brock, Dawn, and Meowth were determined to try.

They were crammed into the Team Rocket hot air balloon, floating toward the Fuego Ironworks as fast as they could.

"Dig it, guys!" Meowth pointed as the factory

came into sight. "Up ahead!"

But the factory wasn't the only thing up ahead. A flock of Pokémon were headed straight for them.

"Golbat!" Brock cried.

"*Oy vey*," Meowth moaned.

Ash was ready for a fight. "Pikachu, help us out!"

"Pachirisu, we need you, too!" Dawn added, tossing out a Poké Ball.

Pachirisu, a blue-and-white Electric-type Pokémon, burst out. The three spikes at the tip of its long tail sizzled with electric charge.

Ash threw out two more Poké Balls. "Staraptor! Gliscor! I choose you!"

Staraptor, a Normal- and Flying-type Pokémon, burst out of its Poké Ball. Pikachu jumped onto its back. Gliscor, a Ground- and Flying-type, stretched its wings and took flight. Pachirisu hopped aboard. They veered toward the Golbat flock.

"Pikachu!" Ash shouted. "Use Thunderbolt, now!"

Pikachu unleashed its Thunderbolt attack. A yellow energy bolt sizzled into the Golbat flock.

"Pachirisu, Discharge!" Dawn cried.

The fluffy little Electric-type Pokémon took aim at the Golbat. The sky blazed with the blue energy of its Discharge attack.

It was too much for the Golbat. They spiraled through the air, out of control. Soon every one had dropped to the ground, out cold.

But Ash knew there was no time to celebrate their triumph. "Let's land over there," he said, pointing to the roof of the factory.

As the balloon landed, a figure stepped out of the shadows.

"Who's that?" Meowth yelped.

It was Jupiter. And she wasn't alone.

# CHAPTER 6

"**S**kuntank, use Flamethrower!" Jupiter ordered. The bulky Poison- and Dark-type raised its tail and shot a wall of fire at the hot air balloon.

Piplup leapt into action. It countered the attack with BubbleBeam. A stream of bubbles collided with Skuntank's gush of fire, turning it to steam.

Ash and his friends climbed out of the balloon before Skuntank could launch another attack. They tried to run, but Jupiter blocked their way.

"You all seem so good at popping up out of nowhere," she said with a taunting smile. "Want to join Team Galactic?"

Dawn wrinkled her nose. "That would be so . . . *ewwwww!*"

Meowth wasn't interested in Jupiter's jokes. He had a team to rescue. "What'd you do

21

with Jessie and James?" he demanded.

"And what about Looker?" Ash added.

Jupiter looked more closely at Ash. Then she peered at Brock and Dawn. Suddenly, she seemed to recognize them — and the smile dropped off of her face. "Oh, Mesprit," she said. Her voice filled with silent fury. "Azelf. Uxie."

Ash and his friends recognized those names. They were the names of the Lake Trio, three mysterious Legendary Pokémon who were said to protect the Sinnoh region. Ash, Brock, and Dawn had seen a vision of them, hovering over their lakes. But how would *Jupiter* know a thing like that? And why would she care?

"Why did it have to be you?" Jupiter asked.

They didn't know what to say.

"I'm talking about the Lake Trio, of course," Jupiter added. Her fists were clenched. Her eyes were narrowed. "Why is it that they chose *you*?"

Ash was confused. "What do you mean, they chose us?"

"You *saw* them!" Jupiter exclaimed. "The Legendary Pokémon they say reside in those lakes!"

Brock decided to get to the bottom of this. "All right," he said. "How do you know about that?"

No one was more confused than Meowth. "Does one of you twerps want to clue me in here? I'm kind of flying blind here."

"We know everything about all of it!" Jupiter told Brock. "The truth of the matter is, *we* were the ones who were supposed to have synchronized with the Lake Trio!"

She signaled to her Golbat. They had recovered enough to launch another attack. The flock veered toward Ash and his friends. But Pikachu and Staraptor swooped in and intercepted them. Pikachu launched another Thunderbolt attack. The Golbat squealed in pain and anger.

Meowth took advantage of the chaos. "You've got a big *mouth*!" he told Jupiter. "Where are Jessie and James? *Tell me!*" His claws glowed as he prepared his Fury Swipes attack.

Jupiter was ready. "Quick, Skuntank. Flamethrower!"

Skuntank extended its deadly tail and shot a thick column of fire at Meowth.

"Piplup, BubbleBeam, let's go!" Dawn cried.

The brave Water-type Pokémon threw itself between Meowth and the wall of fire. Its Bubble-Beam turned the flames into an explosion of steam. The blast threw everyone to the ground.

Gliscor and Staraptor landed just in time. Pikachu and Pachirisu jumped off their backs, prepared for battle.

"Surrounding us, eh?" Jupiter said. She didn't sound worried. "Skuntank, use Toxic, *now*!"

Skuntank spewed out a massive gush of venomous sludge.

"It's toxic!" Brock cried. "Don't breathe it in."

His friends covered their noses and mouths,

trying to avoid the flying gunk. As it spattered onto the roof, it released puffs of poisonous gas.

"Staraptor! Gliscor! Heads up!" Ash warned his Pokémon.

Staraptor wrapped its large wings around Pikachu to shield the smaller Pokémon from the clouds of poison.

It was exactly the distraction Jupiter needed. She ran away.

"Hey, wait!" Brock called.

"That flake flew the coop," Meowth complained.

"The Golbat are gone, too," Brock realized.

In fact, everyone was gone. Moments later, the Team Galactic ship lifted into the air. They were getting away! Pikachu climbed onto Staraptor's back, ready to give chase.

Ash was tempted to let them. But he knew they had something more important to do. "Pikachu and Staraptor, wait a minute," Ash said. "We've gotta check for Team Rocket and Looker first."

Ash was right. But still, no one was very happy to watch the ship disappear into the distance.

Team Galactic had escaped. Again.

Even though she'd gotten away, Jupiter wasn't very happy, either. As the ship carried her off, Jupiter stared out the window, muttering to herself. "I don't get it. Why did the Lake Trio choose them in the first place?"

Across from her, Charon was hunched over a screen. "Jealous of those children, are we?"

"Jealous?" Jupiter rolled her eyes. "Don't be silly. It's not my style."

Charon laughed. "Jealousy is a human emotion, you know."

Jupiter turned the conversation back to business. "Is the Red Chain safe or not?"

"Don't worry," Charon told her. "It's located right below your feet."

Surprised, Jupiter turned her gaze to the trapdoor by her feet. The Red Chain was so close . . . as close as their *destiny*.

She put Ash and the others out of her mind. They weren't important. All that mattered was getting the Red Chain to Cyrus on Mt. Coronet.

Then the real work would begin.

# CHAPTER 7

"Looker!" Ash cried, as they wandered through the abandoned factory.

"Where are you!" Brock shouted. His voice echoed off the high ceilings and rusty equipment.

"Jessie! James!" Meowth yowled. "Report!"

There was no reply.

They wound through one empty corridor after another, but there was no sign of the prisoners. This was beginning to seem hopeless.

But they refused to give up.

All the way on the other side of the factory, Looker and Team Rocket hadn't given up hope, either. But they were beginning to wonder what was going on outside their cell.

"It's gotten awfully quiet out there," Looker said. He peered through the bars. Surely they hadn't just left their prisoners behind?

"My stomach's making tons of noise," Jessie complained.

James sulked. "Starvation simply *stinks*."

"*Shh!*" Looker urged Jessie and James.

The three of them listened hard. They all heard it. Footsteps.

They were getting closer.

"Someone's coming," Looker whispered. He dared another peek through the bars. "It's Ash!"

Dawn spotted him. "It's Looker!"

Brock hurried over. "Are you okay?" he asked.

Meowth joined him impatiently. "All right, do you know where my peeps are?"

"Yes, they're both right here with me," Looker said.

Jessie leapt to her feet. "Meowth!" She had never been so glad to see the cranky Pokémon.

James and Jessie were both so excited that they threw themselves at the door . . . forgetting that it was electrified.

A jolt of electric energy zapped through them. They yelped and twitched, and for a moment they even glowed. Then they were on the ground, buzzing with leftover charge.

"We should've used a sticky note," James said weakly.

Looker felt bad for his fellow prisoners. But there was no time to waste. "All right, Ash and Dawn. Have Pikachu and Piplup launch an attack together so we can break down this door."

"You got it!" Ash said. "Pikachu, Thunderbolt."

"And Piplup, use BubbleBeam," Dawn added.

The Pokémon aimed their attacks at the door. The door blew off its hinges. Looker and Team Rocket were free!

"You helped me out of a tough spot," Looker told Ash and Dawn. "Thank you both."

"No prob," Ash said.

Jessie, James, and Meowth were overjoyed to be together again. They flung their arms around one another.

"It's so good to see you mugs," Meowth said.

"I had faith in you," Jessie told the Pokémon.

"Meowth for the clinch!" James cheered.

But a moment later, their relief faded.

"What's with the fashion freaks?" Jessie asked. She was ready to get some revenge.

"Team Galactic took a powder to parts unknown," Meowth admitted.

"Not for long," said Jessie.

They couldn't stick around, not while Team Galactic was out there somewhere. "*Hasta la vista!*" James called to Looker and Ash.

Meowth hesitated. "I owe you one," he told Ash, Dawn, and Brock. "Big time."

"It's been sublime!" Team Rocket shouted as

a good-bye. Then they ran off. They were determined to find Team Galactic. No one put Team
Rocket behind bars and got away with it.

They hopped into their hot air balloon and took
off. Now where were they supposed to go?

"Sometimes your sense of direction leaves
much to be desired, you know," Jessie complained to Meowth. She wanted Team Galactic
to get found, but it looked more like Team Rocket
was getting lost!

"It's this way, no doubt," Meowth insisted.
He pointed toward a snowy mountain. "Team
Galactic's got nowhere to hide!"

"Well, staying the course will get us to Mt.
Coronet," James said.

"We know those fashion freaks have a fondness
for frolicking in the mountains," Jessie admitted.
"So it's toward the mountains we will go!"

"Coronet, ho!" James shouted.

Meowth couldn't wait. "Yo, yo, *yo!*"

# CHAPTER 8

**B**ack at the Fuego Ironworks, Looker sighed. Even though he was free, he'd still failed in his mission. "So Team Galactic escaped again," he said. "That means my work here is finished. I'd sure like to know what they were working on here."

It couldn't hurt to take one last look around.

Looker led the group deeper into the factory. An elevator carried them several levels beneath the ground. That's where they discovered a laboratory. It was filled with scientific equipment, including two massive steel tanks. They were both empty.

Dawn gaped at the strange surroundings. "What's all this?"

"This wasn't part of the Fuego Ironworks,

that's for sure," Looker said, sounding excited. "It must be Team Galactic's doing!"

He bent over the empty tanks and pulled out a tiny red gem.

"Check it out," Ash said, eagerly. He couldn't believe that Team Galactic had left a clue behind. "Looker, what do you think that is?"

Looker shook his head. He had no idea. None of them did. If they were going to solve this puzzle, they were going to need some help.

So they returned to Floaroma Town, where Officer Jenny was standing by to help them analyze the gem. She took them to a laboratory, where a technician hooked up the gem to a computer.

"That's it," the technician said. "We're ready."

"Now we're able to transmit any data from the object directly to headquarters," Officer Jenny said proudly.

"Thanks for all your hard work," Looker told them. He couldn't wait to see what the analysis revealed.

"So let's begin," the technician said. He

pressed a button. A green beam swept over the gem. Data began to scroll across their screens. It told them what the gem was made of and how it was structured.

But suddenly, the gem began to glow. Then it started to tremble.

The data on the screens vanished. It was replaced by a fuzzy gold mark.

Dawn gasped. She knew that mark.

It was the Team Galactic G.

A moment later, that disappeared, too. The screen filled with Charon's laughing face.

Looker realized what was happening. "No!" he shouted. "Turn it off!" He lunged for the button, but before he could reach it, an explosion of light burst from the gem. The air sizzled with electric charge. It fried every computer in the room.

When the light faded away, Officer Jenny looked around in confusion. She was glad every-one was okay — but what had happened?

Before they could figure it out, the monitor buzzed with an incoming transmission.

"This is the Floaroma Police," Officer Jenny reported into the monitor.

A detective appeared on the screen. He did *not* look happy. "The data you transmitted to International Police Headquarters has wiped our entire database out!" he said angrily.

"And Team Galactic's data?" Looker asked. He was afraid he already knew the answer.

"Apparently it's been destroyed as well," the detective said. "Retrieval uncertain."

Looker couldn't believe he'd been so foolish. "So it was all a trap!"

"That has to be why they left that red object behind," Officer Jenny realized.

Looker nodded. "A warning to stop further investigation . . . or else."

"Whoa, Looker." Ash couldn't believe anyone could be so devious.

"I'll never give up!" Looker exclaimed. He didn't care about the warning. In fact, now he was more determined than ever. "The next time Team Galactic is up to something, I'll be there to stop them!"

35

No one wanted to wait for the next time. They wanted to stop Team Galactic *this* time. But it seemed like there was nothing else they could do.

They left the police station, feeling defeated. As they walked down the steps, Dawn remembered one last thing that didn't make sense. "About those Pokémon, the Lake Trio," she reminded them. "What does it all mean?"

Ash shrugged. "Not sure, since all we did was see them."

"I can't stop wondering how Team Galactic knew about it!" Brock said.

The Lake Trio were crucial to Team Galactic's plan. Even now, Cyrus was at the top of Mt. Coronet, plotting their doom.

"The creation of a new world begins," he said to himself, with an evil smile. "The Spear Key and Spear Pillar, the Adamant Orb and the Lustrous Orb. The Red Chain . . . now all that remains are the three Lake Trio!"

"All preparations for the Galactic Bomb are complete," Saturn told him.

Cyrus's smile widened. "Excellent."

He opened a transmission channel, and a woman with spiky purple hair appeared on his monitor. A dark visor hid her eyes.

Cyrus quickly got down to business. "Sorry to keep you waiting, Pokémon Hunter J. Please proceed with the Lake Trio capture as planned."

Now it was only a matter of time.

# CHAPTER 9

**A**sh, Dawn, and Brock stood in the midst of a strange cloud of mist and stars. They didn't know where they were or how they'd gotten there. But they soon realized they were not alone.

Dawn sucked in a breath as a gray-and-pink Pokémon appeared before her. It hovered in mid-air, its eyes wide and frightened.

"Mesprit," she whispered.

At the same instant, a gray Pokémon with a yellow head appeared before Brock. "Uxie!" he exclaimed.

Ash gazed at the blue Pokémon that floated before him. "Azelf," he said in a soft, awed voice.

Each Pokémon had two long, slender tails that dangled like ropes from its graceful body. The tails were tipped with red jewels. Another red jewel sat at the center of each Pokémon's forehead.

"I'm wondering why you showed yourselves to all of us," Brock said.

"*Uxie*," said Uxie, sounding worried. All three Legendary Pokémon seemed distressed.

"Hey, what's wrong?" Ash asked.

"Tell us," Dawn pleaded. "Is there something that you need to say?"

Again, the Legendary Pokémon didn't answer. They twisted around in horror, as if there was something lurking behind them.

It was a shadow.

A giant, writhing shadow that was growing by the second. The darkness swooped toward them as if it were alive — and hungry.

"That shadow," Ash gasped.

Darkness surrounded them. The Legendary Pokémon fled, but they couldn't escape it.

"Man, this is looking really bad," Ash said, panting as he chased after the Pokémon. He didn't know how he could fight a shadow, but he had to try. The Legendary Pokémon needed him.

But he couldn't outrun the shadow. None of them could. The darkness wrapped itself around the Legendary Pokémon. Ash lunged toward them, desperate, and then —

He woke up.

Ash sucked in a deep breath. Sweat poured down his face. His heart thumped in his chest. It felt so *real*.

Even though it was the middle of the night, Dawn and Brock were awake, too. Their faces were pale.

"What a dream," Dawn said in a hushed voice. "I just saw the Legendary Pokémon."

"That shadow?" Brock asked, surprised. "Yeah. Me, too!"

Ash's jaw dropped open. "Did we have the same dream?"

It wasn't possible . . . was it?

⊙ ⊙ ⊙ ⊙ ⊙

What Ash didn't know was that the Legendary Pokémon were in serious trouble — in real life. While he, Brock, and Dawn were comparing their dreams, Hunter J's ship was powering toward Azelf's home.

"We're now above Lake Valor," her henchman reported as they arrived.

"Descend to five hundred meters," Hunter J ordered him. "Prepare to drop Galactic Bomb!"

On the underbelly of the ship, big doors swung open. The Galactic Bomb descended. A metal claw attached it to the ship — but not for long.

Down below, Pokémon Trainer Gary Oak was walking along the lake with his Dark-type Pokémon, Umbreon. It was black with golden stripes and a golden circle on its forehead — and it could sense that something wasn't right. At the sound of thunder, it looked up toward the sky. But that wasn't thunder.

It was Hunter J's ship.

Alarmed, Gary pulled out his walkie-talkie.

"Come in, Professor Rowan," he said. "This is Gary at Lake Valor. Pokémon Hunter J has appeared!"

The Professor could see the ship on the screen of his wall monitor. He frowned. "I'm certain that she's come for the Legendary Pokémon," he said. The Professor turned to his assistant. "All right, then, get in touch with Yuzo at Lake Verity and Carolina at Lake Acuity." That was where the other two Legendary Pokémon lived. Professor Rowan feared they might be in trouble, too.

Once he alerted Professor Rowan, Gary got ready for battle. It was his job to protect the Pokémon on Lake Valor, no matter what it took. "Umbreon, let's *go*!" he cried. Then he tossed out a Poké Ball. "Electivire — come on out, too!"

The yellow-and-black striped Electric-type Pokémon burst out of its Poké Ball. But it turned out Hunter J wasn't the only threat. Before Gary could tell his Pokémon to attack, he heard a voice behind him. It was Saturn — along with two Team Galactic henchmen and Toxicroak.

Before Gary could react, Saturn shouted, "Toxicroak, use Dark Pulse!"

The Poison- and Fighting-type Pokémon roared. A dark purple blast shot through the air.

"Oh, no!" Gary cried. "Electivire!"

The Electric-type Pokémon managed to block the attack.

"Get out!" Saturn told Gary. He was enraged that anyone would try to challenge him.

"You're Team Galactic, huh?" Gary said, trying not to sound afraid. "Well, I'm not gonna stand by and let you go. Umbreon, use Psychic!"

Umbreon's eyes began to glow. The air around it pulsed with its Psychic attack.

"Toxicroak, use X-Scissor," Saturn ordered.

Toxicroak charged, slashing its sharp red claws. Its attack was too strong. Umbreon went flying. It landed on the ground with a thud.

"Umbreon!" Gary cried in alarm.

But the Pokémon didn't move.

# CHAPTER 10

"**S**ir, we've arrived at the drop point," Hunter J's henchman informed her.

Right on time. Hunter J smiled. "Release the Galactic Bomb."

Beneath the ship, the metal claw opened, and the bomb dropped toward the lake. It plunged into the water with a mighty splash. The bomb rocketed toward the bottom of the lake, zooming deeper and deeper and deeper . . . until it exploded.

As the lake was rocked by an enormous energy blast, Azelf screamed in pain.

Far away in Floaroma Town, Ash screamed, too.

"Hey, Ash," Dawn said. "What's wrong?"

They were sitting at the kitchen table having a snack. But now Ash was grabbing his head like he was in pain.

"Are you okay?" Brock asked.

Ash stared at them in wonder. "I felt it. It's *Azelf*!"

Dawn was shocked. "You mean, like the dream?"

Brock frowned. "If that's true, then what *was* that dream?" He was more certain than ever: It hadn't been a dream at all.

They decided to call Professor Rowan and tell him what had happened.

"I can't believe you all felt something!" he exclaimed.

"I knew it," Dawn said. "Something *did* happen."

"Team Galactic and Pokémon Hunter J have arrived at Lake Valor," the professor told them. "Gary is there attempting to fend them off."

"Gary *Oak*?" Ash asked, surprised to hear that his old friend was involved.

Professor Rowan nodded, then transmitted an image of what was happening at the lake.

"It's J!" Ash said, when he saw the ship hovering over Lake Valor.

"So Team Galactic's joined forces with J," Brock said.

Dawn was worried for the little blue Pokémon who lived in the lake. "And they're after Azelf!"

The Galactic Bomb had turned Lake Valor into a swirling vortex. It glowed with energy, shooting beams of light into the sky.

Back at the shore, Gary was frozen at the sight of the vortex. "It — it can't be!"

A glowing ball of energy rose slowly from the lake and hovered overhead.

"I'll enlighten you," Saturn said. "The Galactic Bomb — made out of the meteorite taken from Veilstone City — is powerful enough to open up a hole in space!"

Gary couldn't believe what he was hearing.

"You see, the Lake Pokémon don't exactly live in a lake, as it were," Saturn continued. "The truth is the Lake Pokémon simply observe our world from another dimension through a portal that looks very much like a lake!"

Safe in his laboratory, Professor Rowan watched the attack on his monitor. His screen showed the same glowing vortex forming at Lake Verity. Then Yuzo, the monitor there, checked in with bad news. "Professor Rowan, this is Yuzo here, confirming abnormal activity at Lake Verity," he reported.

"Understood," Rowan said sadly. He'd been afraid this would happen. The Legendary Pokémon had been created during the very beginnings of the universe. They worked in close harmony protecting Sinnoh. Legend stated that if one of them were to fall, the other two would have to appear to restore balance.

"Professor!" Rowan's assistant called. "There's an incoming transmission from Carolina."

Professor Carolina, stationed at Lake Acuity, didn't have any better news to report. "It's happening here as well," she said. "Is it those kids again?"

"Yes," Rowan told her. "It would appear that the Legendary Pokémon are sending some sort of signal to Ash and his friends."

It was a distress signal, because Azelf and the other Legendary Pokémon were in some serious trouble. Unfortunately, Ash and his friends were too far away to help. Gary was brave, but he was also outnumbered.

"Electivire, use Thunder!" he ordered.

The Electric-type Pokémon threw its Thunder attack at Toxicroak, but Toxicroak fended off the blow. It shot out a Poison Jab in return. Electivire toppled to the ground.

"Electivire!" Gary shouted.

"You stay out of this," Saturn warned him.

The Team Galactic henchmen tossed up handfuls of Poké Balls, and the sky filled with Golbat.

As Gary watched, helpless to prevent it, Hunter J released Salamence. The giant Dragon- and Flying-type Pokémon swooped into the air, with Hunter J perched on its back.

They flew toward the glowing ball of energy that hovered about the lake. But it wasn't just energy — it was *Azelf*, in a sphere of light.

"Salamence, Hyper Beam," Hunter J ordered.

The attack slammed into Azelf.

In Floaroma Town, Ash cringed in pain again. "It's Azelf!" he cried. But there was nothing he could do.

The glowing energy surrounding Azelf got even brighter. Then it vanished. Azelf was left floating in the sky, without any protection.

The flock of Golbat swarmed.

"Use Supersonic!" Saturn called to them.

As the Supersonic attack shook the sky, Azelf tried to fight back. It launched a powerful Confusion attack. One by one, the Golbat dropped out of the sky.

But Azelf wasn't safe yet. Hunter J was waiting. She fired her immobilizing beam at Azelf.

The Legendary Pokémon struggled to release another Confusion attack, but Hunter J's beam overpowered it. The beam froze the Pokémon. It became stiff and lifeless as a stone. Which made it easy for Hunter J to swoop in and trap it under a dome of glass.

"Azelf!" Gary cried from the shore.

The glass dome floated toward the ground. It landed gently in Saturn's outstretched hands. Gary rushed toward him, desperate to help Azelf. But Purugly and Skuntank lumbered into his way.

Gary froze in his tracks.

Before the Team Galactic Pokémon could strike, two golden energy balls appeared in the sky. It was Uxie and Mesprit, the other two Legendary Pokémon!

Mars gazed at them in shock. "It's just as Cyrus said it would be! If one falls, then the rest come tumbling down, too."

"What does *that* mean?" Gary wondered.

He was about to find out.

"Now, Golbat!" Mars and Jupiter shouted together. "Supersonic!"

The sky filled with deafening Supersonic sound waves. Uxie and Mesprit dodged the attack as best they could. But they couldn't escape Hunter J and Salamence.

The Legendary Pokémon shot two brilliant beams of light toward Hunter J.

"It looks like they both used Future Sight at once!" Saturn exclaimed.

With Future Sight, the Legendary Pokémon could send their attack through time. Which meant in the near future, Hunter J would be in big trouble.

But for now, there was nothing to stop her from aiming her wrist cannon at Uxie and Mesprit. The immobilizing beam slammed into them. In seconds, both were petrified and trapped under glass.

"What have you done?" Gary moaned, as Team Galactic loaded their Pokémon prisoners onto their ship.

They ignored him.

"Excellent work, Pokémon Hunter J," Mars

said, as the Pokémon hunter landed safely. "I hope you're not hurt."

"See, we couldn't just let ourselves be pushed around by the Lake Trio," Jupiter added. She had emerged from the ship to help tend to the Poké-mon. "We *are* the chosen ones, after all."

"Hunter J, well done!" Saturn put in. "You have your payment, as agreed."

Once she was paid, Hunter J had nothing left to say to Team Galactic. She climbed back on Salamence. The Pokémon flew her back to her ship.

"Ready for departure?" she asked.

"We're ready, sir," the pilot said.

"All right. Return to base!"

He powered up the engines. But before they could go anywhere, two jagged beams of energy smashed into the ship. The engines burst into flame.

It had to be Mesprit and Uxie's Future Sight attacks!

Hunter J struggled to keep the ship in the air. "Increase engines to max power!" she shouted. "Maintain our speed!"

Smoke billowed into the bridge. The ship bucked and shuddered beneath their feet. Crew members raced back and forth, patching up equipment and putting out fires. But the ship was falling out of the sky.

"Engines losing power *fast!*" one crew member shouted.

"We've lost control!" added another, terrified.

The ship crashed into the lake. Windows exploded as water gushed into the ship. It sank quickly, and then exploded. Pokémon Hunter J's ship had taken its last flight.

The Legendary Pokémon had gotten their revenge on Pokémon Hunter J. But they were still trapped. Which meant Team Galactic was one step closer to achieving its evil plan.

And Ash, Brock, and Dawn had felt every minute of it. They were connected to the Legendary Trio. The pain the Pokémon felt was their pain, too. They knew they had to do *something* to save Azelf, Uxie, and Mesprit.

But what?

# CHAPTER 11

The Team Rocket balloon floated over the mountains. Jessie and James scanned the countryside, searching for their prey. They were beginning to lose hope. Would they *ever* track down Team Galactic?

James peered through his binoculars. "Wall-to-wall rock, and not a pebble more," he reported.

"And no Team Galactic to even the score," Jessie complained.

Meowth was sulking. "This is one stinkin' bore," he whined. Suddenly, he spotted something. "Wait!" he yelped, pointing toward the nearest mountain peak. "Check out that rocky floor!"

"Where, what for?" Jessie asked.

"Say, it's lunch box guy!" James cried happily. Not long ago, Looker had run into them on a train and given them boxed lunches when they were hungry. (Team Rocket was *always* hungry.) They had called him "lunch box guy" ever since.

They brought the balloon in for a landing. "Lunch box guyyyyy!" they shrieked together.

"*Shhh!*" Looker urged them. He was hiding behind a giant boulder, spying on Team Galactic. "Excuse me, my code name is Looker."

"That's nice," Jessie said. "But to us —"

"You're the boss of boxed lunches," James finished.

Looker snorted. "Whatever. Meanwhile, Team Galactic's on a Mt. Coronet watch. It's even possible they might have already spotted us here."

"So you're looking for them, too?" James asked. "What a coincidence."

"Of course!" Looker said. "After what they did to me before? I've got to figure out what they're up to here and put a stop to it — if only to restore my pristine reputation."

"We'll help you," James promised.

Looker didn't seem very grateful.

"We're experts at world peace and beating up jerks," Meowth pointed out.

"Team Rocket in your face!" the three of them cheered.

Looker sighed. It looked like he was going to have some help in this mission — whether he wanted it or not.

Back in Floaroma Town, Ash, Dawn, and Brock were eager to help, too. They contacted Professor Rowan, begging him to protect the Legendary Pokémon.

"I know how you feel," he said. "But I'm afraid it's too late!"

"Professor, wait," Ash said, before the Professor could hang up. "We have to do something to help them out!"

"Right!" Dawn agreed. "We think the Pokémon are pleading with us to save them all, *now.*"

"We got to go!" Brock added. If the Professor didn't know how to help the Pokémon, they would find another way. They ran outside.

At that moment, Pokémon Champion Cynthia's off-road vehicle pulled up. Cynthia was a friend of Ash, Dawn, and Brock's. "All right, hop in!" she called to the gang.

They hopped into the back and took off down the road as fast as they could. As they drove, Ash, Brock, and Dawn could feel the Legendary Trio calling to them. Would they get there in time to help — wherever *there* was?

"If you want to help them out, you'll have to take care of Team Galactic," Cynthia told them. "You're all familiar with Looker, aren't you?"

"Yeah, we are — from the International Police," Dawn said. "What about him?"

"He's on Mt. Coronet investigating," Cynthia

explained. "We're going to meet him now."

As they drove, they contacted Professor Rowan for an update.

"I've asked Officer Jenny to check on the status of the entire area," he reported.

"Do you have any idea where Team Galactic might have gone, Professor?" Dawn asked.

"No," he admitted. "But I'll be sure to pass along any information as it becomes available. Cynthia — and you kids as well — be careful."

"Yes, we will," Cynthia promised.

Brock leaned forward to talk to the others. "So, I guess now we wait." It wasn't his favorite thing to do at a time like this.

Cynthia looked thoughtful. "Do you remember the mural in the Celestic Ruins?" she asked.

"Yeah!" Ash and his friends said.

It was a mural of the Lake Trio. Back when they first saw it, they'd never imagined they might actually meet the Legendary Pokémon face-to-face.

"As of this moment, Team Galactic has the Lake Trio and the two treasures in its possession," Cynthia said. "Which looks to me like they're fully prepared to call forth Dialga and Palkia."

Ash and his friends weren't sure what she meant.

"Of course, Dialga is known as the Ruler of Time," Cynthia explained, "and Palkia is known as the Ruler of Space. But for two Legendary Pokémon like them to fall under human control is beyond comprehension!" She looked horrified at the thought. "Why, Team Galactic might be able to unleash ancient powers that we're not even aware of!"

Cynthia had no idea how right she was. At that very moment, the Lake Trio were imprisoned in Team Galactic's base. They hung suspended in three vats of liquid.

Cyrus looked down on them with pleasure. "Now, begin!" he commanded his team.

Charon stood before a bank of computers. At Cyrus's order, he flipped a large switch. "It's time to see . . . the power of the Red Chain!"

Three red gems were lowered into the three vats of liquid. As they made contact with the Lake Trio, the gems began to glow. Slowly, they merged with the gems in the Legendary Pokémon's foreheads. The Pokémon began to glow, too.

In the truck with Cynthia, Ash grabbed his head. His face twisted in pain.

"You're feeling it again?" Cynthia asked.

Ash could barely speak. He finally managed to force out the words, "It *hurts!*"

Dawn was too weak to move. "It's so intense," she murmured.

Brock's head was pounding. He couldn't think. "Much stronger than before!"

Cynthia turned to them, searching for words that would comfort Ash and his friends. But before she could speak . . . they vanished!

The vehicle skidded to a stop. Cynthia gaped at the empty seats. "It can't be! They've been . . . *summoned.*"

# CHAPTER 12

"There, you see?" Charon asked gleefully, as the Lake Trio continued to glow. "Yes, the Veil-stone Meteorite was most definitely created from the core substance of the universe! Filled with a power that we have now tapped into —"

He stopped talking abruptly as Ash, Dawn, and Brock materialized in the middle of the room.

Team Galactic looked shocked.

The kids looked confused.

But Charon just laughed. "Well, could it be? Looks like we've got company!"

Ash swept his eyes over the laboratory equipment, Charon, and the rest of Team Galactic. Then he spotted the imprisoned Pokémon.

"Azelf!" he cried.

Dawn noticed them, too. "Mesprit!"

"Uxie!" Brock said. "The three of them must have brought us here."

Ash turned to Team Galactic, furious. "All right, what've you all done?" he demanded.

Team Galactic wasn't interested in giving out answers. They preferred to fight.

"Toxicroak's looking forward to seeing you," Saturn said happily.

He tossed up a Poké Ball, and Toxicroak burst out.

"Skuntank, now," Jupiter said, calling the Poison- and Dark-type Pokémon. "Let's do this!"

"Purugly, we need your help, too," Mars called. The Normal-type Pokémon cinched its waist with its forked tail, ready for battle.

Ash wasn't afraid. "You ready, Pikachu?"

The little Electric-type Pokémon wasn't afraid, either.

"You're not ready for *us*," Mars and Jupiter jeered.

"Toxicroak, time for *fun*," Saturn cheered.

The two groups faced off, poised to attack. But before they could, Cyrus appeared in the doorway.

"Hold on!" he commanded. He didn't seem at all surprised that Ash and his friends were on board. "No fighting allowed."

Ash couldn't believe his eyes. "Cyrus? *Here*?"

Cyrus was a wealthy businessman who had built many of the Sinnoh region's tallest buildings. Ash and his friends had met him before, but he had pretended that he wanted to *help* Pokémon, not use their powers for evil.

"I don't get it," Dawn said.

Brock did. "That must mean you're part of Team Galactic!"

"So that's how Jupiter knew we'd seen the Lake Trio! *You* told them," said Ash, scowling. They had trusted Cyrus — and he had betrayed them.

Cyrus just smiled. "Fighting is by far the most frightful by-product of the human heart," he said. "Haven't I been telling you that time and time again?" he asked his henchmen.

"Sir!" Saturn agreed. He wanted to fight. But he couldn't defy his leader.

Jupiter cleared her throat nervously. "But since these children pose a very real threat to our plan for a new world order . . . isn't it only natural to eliminate them?"

Cyrus quieted her with a glare. "Behold!" he announced. "This is just the kind of accomplishment the human heart has the potential to achieve. But when your heart is ruled by emotions, you will but fight. In which case humanity will never advance."

Cyrus turned to Ash and his friends. "I guess I could let you know what this is about," he told them. "I *am* part of this. Team Galactic is my creation — and you are now in my creation's headquarters!"

"Headquarters?" Ash asked. "In *here*?"

"Correct," Cyrus said. "We're bringing about the dawn of a new world order. So we're gathered here to discard the old world of discord and con-flict and make a much better one in place of it!"

For Ash, the pieces were finally starting to fall into place. "So it was *you* who stole the Lustrous Orb from the Celestic Ruins. You lied to all of us!"

"Lose your rage," Cyrus suggested. "It only destroys."

"No way!" Dawn said. Her rage was just get-ting started. "Not when you treat Pokémon that way. This has got to stop. Now let them go back to their lakes!"

"That can't be done," Cyrus informed her. "They're quite necessary for us to be able to bring forth the new world."

Brock gasped. "Then that means it's exactly as Cynthia said it was!"

Cyrus saw there was no point in trying to convince the kids to go along with him. He turned to his henchmen. "Obviously, these children must mean something important if the Legendary

Pokémon saw fit to bring them all here. We will need to keep them around until our task is completed, just in case."

At his command, Team Galactic closed in on Ash, Brock, and Dawn.

"You won't get away with it!" Ash shouted. "Who cares if you're Team Galactic?" He couldn't take his eyes off the imprisoned Pokémon. Even if he was outnumbered and surrounded, he had to at least try. "Pikachu! Thunderbolt! Let's *go*!"

"Piplup, use BubbleBeam," Dawn ordered.

"Croagunk, do it!" Brock added.

Team Galactic prepared themselves for the attack. But the Pokémon weren't aiming at them. Instead, they aimed at the vats imprisoning the Lake Trio.

Pikachu's energy beam and Piplup's stream of bubbles smashed into the vats containing the Lake Trio. Their prisons burst into pieces. The Lake Trio was free!

But Team Galactic wasn't going to let them go without a fight.

"Purugly!" Mars commanded her Pokémon.

"Skuntank!" Jupiter called hers to action.

"Iron Tail, now!" Mars told Purugly. The attack slammed into Ash, Brock, and Dawn. They sailed through the air and landed in a heap.

"Sludge Bomb," Saturn said quickly. "Go!"

Skuntank attacked. A gush of black slime arced through the air, splattering Ash, his friends, and their three Pokémon. Pikachu, Piplup, and Croagunk flew backward into their Trainers' arms.

The kids had no choice. They couldn't fight any longer — their wounded Pokémon needed time to heal.

*At least we freed the Lake Trio*, Ash thought.

There was just one problem: The Lake Trio wasn't trying to escape. In fact, they weren't doing anything but hovering in the air over Cyrus's head. The gems in their foreheads were glowing.

"Azelf, oh man, what's wrong?" Ash asked.

"Mesprit, don't you recognize us?" Dawn said pleadingly.

Cyrus grinned and raised a fist in the air. He opened his fingers to reveal another red gem at the center of his palm.

"We have the Red Chain, which now possesses the Powers of the Original One," he crowed. "So as you can see, they are now under my *complete control*!"

"Original One?" Ash echoed in confusion.

"According to legend, these powers are responsible for reshaping our entire world," Charon explained. "Which means that no Pokémon is able to withstand them!"

That's when Ash understood. The Lake Trio wasn't free at all. They were Team Galactic's slaves.

"It is with these Original Powers that I will create a new world order!" Cyrus roared. There was madness in his eyes.

"You're out of your mind!" Ash shot back.

"You can't do that!" Dawn yelled.

Cyrus acted like they hadn't spoken. "Make certain you take care of those children," he told Saturn. Then he spun on his heel and stalked out. The Lake Trio floated behind him.

"Come back here!" Ash called. But neither Cyrus nor the Legendary Pokémon listened.

The Team Galactic henchmen closed in. They forced Ash, Brock, and Dawn out of their base and into their ship, locking the three Trainers in. Ash and the others were trapped in a large, empty space with steel walls. Their hands were tied behind their backs. There was no way out.

"What's going to happen to us now?" Dawn asked, frightened.

"Cyrus is using us as hostages so Uxie and the others will do what he tells them to," Brock guessed. "We're part of his backup plan, in case the Lake Trio breaks free from his control."

Ash was worried for himself and his friends. But not as worried as he was for the Lake Trio. "We've gotta get out of here!" he said urgently. "Those Pokémon came to see us in our dreams!"

"And they did it because they were asking us for our help," Dawn said. "So we *can't* let them down."

Everyone agreed. They had to help the Legendary Pokémon. Which meant they had to escape.

Somehow.

# CHAPTER 13

Looker and Team Rocket were still spying on Team Galactic. They had found the large stone gateway carved into the mountain. Several guards marched back and forth, protecting the entrance.

"Dear me," James said. "My innate fashion-sensing instincts are telling me Team Galactic must be on the premises!"

"Look at the size of that security detail," Jessie said. "No doubt they've got a state-of-the-art hideout."

Meowth was sick of waiting. He was ready for some action. "Let's hit 'em where they hide!"

But Looker was cautious. "Slow it down," he urged them. "We need to secure the area first."

Team Rocket didn't like that one bit. "Policeman party pooper!" they jeered. Jessie and James pulled a pair of Team Galactic uniforms out of their bag and pulled them on over their clothes.

"When it comes to disguises, we at Team Rocket are like no other," James bragged.

"And we mean that in a *good* way," Meowth said, just in case there was any doubt.

"Of course, you're not the only ones —" said Looker, "— when it comes to master of disguise!" He whipped out a Team Galactic costume.

Soon, everyone was in costume. It was time to strike.

"Remember, we have to be careful," Looker warned Team Rocket. "Our goal is to take control of Team Galactic's base, and then find a way to get in contact with Cynthia."

"Well, here goes nothing!" Jessie peeked out from behind the boulder. The Team Galactic guards had their backs to her. Jessie threw a Poké Ball. "All right, Yanmega. Use Silver Wind!"

The dark green Bug- and Flying-type Pokémon buzzed toward the Team Galactic guards and attacked. The guards didn't know what hit them.

Soon they were all on the ground, their heads spinning.

Looker, Jessie, and James rushed over to tie them up. They dragged the guards behind the boul-
der and took their place in front of the stone gateway. In their Team Galactic disguises, they were sure to blend right in.

And just in time! There was a roaring thunder overhead, and the Team Galactic ship appeared in the sky. It came in for a landing.

"They're here!" Looker said. "Most likely with Team Galactic's leader onboard."

"About time we met face-to-face," James said.

"Destroying those fashion freaks has been high on my to-do list," Jessie said.

"Yeah, me, too!" Meowth added.

The ship landed, and several members of Team Galactic climbed out. Jessie, James, and Looker stood stiffly at attention. They hoped their disguises would work.

When Looker spotted Cyrus, his eyes widened. "I know that man," he whispered.

Jessie recognized him, too. "That big mouth gave a speech —"

"— back at the Celestic Ruins!" James remembered.

Meowth couldn't believe it. "*He's* the Team Galactic big cheese?"

They weren't the only ones who'd spotted a familiar face. Team Galactic took one look and recognized *them*!

Jupiter glared. "All right, Skuntank, use Flamethrower. Let's go!"

A wall of flame slammed into them. When it faded away, their disguises had burned to ash.

"How could they tell?" Looker asked weakly. He looked as if he were about to faint.

"They *couldn't* know who we are," Jessie said. She, too, looked weak.

"My *mother* wouldn't've known me in this disguise!" James murmured. A moment later, he was out cold — along with Jessie and Looker.

When they woke up, they found themselves in a storage hold — with Ash, Brock, and Dawn! Jupiter stood in the doorway, blocking their escape.

"Hey, look, it's Team Rocket," Ash said in surprise.

"Yeah, and Looker's with them," Dawn added.

Looker had hoped to see his friends again — but he was sorry to see them *here*. "They've gotten you, too?"

Brock jerked his head toward Team Rocket. "Why are you here with *them*?" he asked.

As he spoke, Jupiter slammed the door shut. They were prisoners yet again.

"Wait!" Ash shouted. He slammed against the door. "Open the door! Let us out of here!"

There was no response.

⊙　⊙　⊙　⊙　⊙

Jupiter joined Cyrus at the stone gateway.

"The Spear Key," Cyrus requested.

At his command, Saturn opened a silver briefcase. Inside lay a glowing golden lattice. It floated toward the stone gateway, and the golden globe at its center. When the globe and the lattice made contact, the stone gave way to a gateway of pure energy. Cyrus pressed his hand to the globe, and the doors parted. Beyond them lay a staircase made of light. It led into the deep, deep darkness.

"Spear Pillar must be deep within that passageway," Charon said.

Cyrus nodded. "Exactly as it was written in ancient times."

They entered the darkness. All but Jupiter. She was left behind to keep an eye on the prisoners. And she was none too happy about it. "*Awww*, why do *I* have to stay behind and guard this thing, anyway?" she complained.

She was so busy sulking that she didn't notice Garchomp swooping down until it slammed right into Skuntank. The Poison-and-Dark-type Pokémon toppled over.

"Skuntank!" Alarmed, Jupiter knelt by the wounded Pokémon as Cynthia's truck skidded to a stop before her. The Pokémon Champion was never far from her Garchomp.

Cynthia hopped out of the truck. Jupiter leapt to her feet.

"I know *you*." She pulled out a Poké Ball. But before she could open it, Garchomp returned, and this time, the spiky Dragon-and-Ground-type Pokémon was ready for Jupiter.

"Now, where are they?" Cynthia asked.

A few moments later, Cynthia had found her friends. She pried open the doors and set them free.

"Cynthia!" cried Ash.

"It's the Champion!" Looker said in surprise.

"Thanks for getting in touch with me," Cynthia told Looker. If he hadn't, she would never have known where to find them.

Quickly, the former prisoners tied up Jupiter. They found the other guards that Cyrus had left behind and tied them up, too.

"Don't feel very fashionable *now*, do you?" James taunted them.

"There's nothing like a little payback," Jessie preened. "Time to soothe the savage ego."

Jupiter was fuming. "It's too late," she told them. "The world as you know it is going to end."

"We'll see about that," Ash said. "You guys are through! Forget it!"

"The Legendary Pokémon don't want anything to do with you, either," Dawn said.

Looker and Team Rocket decided to stay behind and guard Jupiter. But Ash, Brock, Dawn, and Cynthia had to find Cyrus and stop him from whatever he was about to do.

Which meant stepping through the gateway — no matter what was waiting for them in the darkness.

# CHAPTER 14

Cyrus led his team through the dark passage. Glowing silver pillars along the path lit their way. It felt like they had been walking forever when they finally reached the treasure.

A cluster of pillars surrounded a massive stone triangle. A pedestal sprouted from each point, and two more stood at the very center.

"So that's the Spear Pillar, eh?" Charon said. "In perfect shape after all these years!"

Cyrus summoned the Lake Trio. He placed each of them on a pedestal at the three points of the triangle. Then he told Saturn and Mars to put the Adamant and Lustrous Orbs on the pedestals at the center.

"Azelf, Mesprit, and Uxie, hear me now!" Cyrus boomed. "Transfer your ancient powers to the

Adamant and Lustrous Orbs. And using the infinite Original Powers, connect time and space!"

The Legendary Pokémon had to obey. They glowed red as the energy flowed through them and into the orbs.

"And, fire!" Charon shouted, setting off a cannon. It shot out two loops of Red Chain. They spiraled through the air over the Spear Pillar, and the energy swirled through them.

Above Mt. Coronet, the sky began churning in a whirlpool of dark clouds. Day turned to night.

The Red Chains glowed brighter and brighter.

"Fascinating!" Charon exclaimed. "Quite an impressive level of energy!"

Cyrus raised his fist and opened his fingers. The red gem embedded in his palm shot a bright beam at the swirls of energy.

"Dialga and Palkia, the time has come," Cyrus said. "*Now!* Reveal yourselves!"

Slowly, the swirls of energy resolved into two giant, ghostly Pokémon. One was blue, one red. Both shimmered, as if made of stars.

Both were trapped in place by a loop of Red Chain.

Saturn gasped in awe. "We are witnessing the Original Powers."

There was a long moment of silence as Team Galactic gazed up at the powerful Pokémon they had dragged into this dimension.

Then the silence turned to chaos. Pikachu, Piplup, Staraptor, Croagunk, Gliscor, and Garchomp burst into the passageway. Ash, Brock, Dawn, and Cynthia weren't far behind.

Cynthia stared at the two Legendary Pokémon. "Dialga, Palkia, and the three Legendary Lake Guardians," she breathed. "I've always wanted to meet them all . . . but certainly not like *this*!"

"Stop it, Cyrus!" Ash cried.

Charon was furious. "You kids just don't know when to quit!"

"I've had enough," Mars growled. "Purugly, *now*." She tossed out her Poké Balls.

Purugly charged, while a swarm of Golbat swooped toward Ash.

"Quick, Pikachu, use Thunderbolt!" he yelled.

"Piplup, use BubbleBeam!" Dawn ordered.

Golbat and Purugly were down for the count!

"Here's our chance to save the Lake Guardians," Cynthia cried. "Quick!"

"You heard that?" Ash asked the Pokémon.

They had. So they sprang into action. Pikachu, Staraptor, Piplup, Gliscor, Croagunk, and Garchomp zoomed at Team Galactic.

Team Galactic didn't stand a chance. They ducked as Pikachu, Piplup, and Croagunk ran toward the Lake Trio. Together, the three Pokémon smashed the control jewels on the Lake Trio's foreheads. Then Ash, Brock, and Dawn swooped in and grabbed Azelf, Mesprit, and Uxie.

"Azelf, it's *me*," Ash said. "Are you okay?"

"I've got you," Dawn said. Mesprit was limp in her arms. "It's *me*."

"I'm coming!" Brock promised. But Uxie didn't seem to recognize him. "It's *Brock*."

Once the Lake Trio were off the pedestals, Dialga and Palkia faded away.

"They're both disappearing!" Saturn cried.

"You showed Cyrus," Ash told his Pokémon, as he returned them to their Poké Balls. "What do you think of *that*?" he taunted Cyrus.

"You no longer have the power to control Dialga or Palkia," Cynthia told him.

"I wouldn't be so sure. . . ." Cyrus raised his fist again, wielding the red gem. At his command, Dialga and Palkia appeared. This time, it wasn't their ghostly forms — it was really them!

Dialga and Palkia screamed and writhed, trying to escape from the Red Chain. But it was no use.

Cyrus was *still* in control!

"They can't resist," Saturn cackled. "It's impossible to break free from the Red Chain that contains the Original Powers."

"What's happening to them?" Dawn asked.

"It has to be those rings," Cynthia guessed, pointing to the Red Chain.

Without warning, the Legendary Pokémon's eyes began to glow. Azelf slipped out of Ash's arms and floated before him. Uxie and Mesprit did the same.

"What's going on?" Ash asked.

Sweat trickled down Dawn's forehead. "It's so warm," she said.

Brock was getting a strange, tingling feeling.

"They must be *willing* this to happen," he realized.

The Lake Trio stared intensely at the kids, as if they were trying to tell them something.

Ash closed his eyes. A voice spoke to him, deep in his mind. Though he'd never heard it before, he recognized it immediately. It was *Azelf's* voice.

"Whoa, I can hear them," he said. "They're asking us to help save Dialga and Palkia!"

"Wow, I can hear them, too!" Dawn exclaimed. "I can really hear them, Cynthia."

The Champion smiled. "Your hearts have become one with the Legendary Pokémon. It's truly a wonderful thing."

Cyrus ignored them all. He couldn't be bothered to deal with such nuisances anymore. Not when he was so close to his goal.

"Dialga, Ruler of Time! Palkia, Ruler of Space! Release your powers now," he commanded them. "Create a new universe before me!"

Dialga and Palkia let loose a mighty roar. Energy flowed from their open mouths.

"Get away!" Cynthia screamed, as the beams combined into a swirling sphere. Ash, Dawn, and Brock dove for safety as the sphere expanded. Stars swirled within it.

It really was a new universe, just as Cyrus had always dreamed.

"Our new world," he whispered. "And it's about to be born!" He stepped before the swirling universe. "I am the one who is finally going to bring order to this chaos!"

"I won't let you!" Ash shouted.

"Aim for the chains, Ash," Cynthia advised. "If we can release Dialga and Palkia, we might be able to stop the creation of the new world."

Ash clenched his fists. "Then let's *do* this.

Pikachu, use Thunderbolt."

"Piplup, use BubbleBeam," Dawn told the little blue Pokémon. "Now!"

"Croagunk, Poison Sting!" Brock shouted.

"Use Draco Meteor!" Cynthia ordered her trusty Garchomp.

The combined force of their attacks rained down on the Red Chain. It was working! The Chain was weakening.

"Dialga, use Roar of Time!" Cyrus commanded. "Palkia, use Spacial Rend."

Ash and his friends froze in terror as Dialga and Palkia unleashed their most powerful attacks. But the Lake Trio wouldn't let harm come to their friends. They threw themselves in the path of the attack, creating a protective energy shield around Ash and his friends. The Roar of Time and Spacial Rend attacks bounced right off the shield.

"We're okay!" Ash said in surprise as the energy faded away and he was still in one piece.

"You did that for *us*?" Dawn asked the Legend-ary Pokémon.

"Thanks, you three!" Brock said.

Mars decided it might be time to get out of there before the Legendary Pokémon decided to get a little revenge. "Oh, please, Cyrus, sir," she begged. "Let's go to our new world right away."

"I have no need for *you*," Cyrus sneered. "Your very existence will poison my new world."

Saturn gasped. "No need for . . . us?"

"This new world belongs to me alone!" Cyrus roared. "You could never understand what it truly means." He turned his back on his team and gazed at the galaxies swirling in his new universe.

"Let's attack those rings once more," Cynthia suggested quietly. There *had* to be a way to break the Red Chain.

"Right, let's do it, now," Ash agreed.

Dawn turned to the Lake Trio. "Help us, please!"

At her pleading, Azelf, Mesprit, and Uxie combined attacks and aimed them at the Red Chain. The rings sizzled and shook under the power of the attack — and then dissolved into smoke.

Dialga and Palkia fell to the ground. The universe they had created began to shrink.

"They're vanishing now," Charon said. "So I guess this is the end."

Cyrus refused to let it happen. He'd worked too hard, for too long. "This is *my* perfect world," he said, striding toward the glowing universe. "Governed by an order that does not require either heart or conscience —"

"Cyrus, stop!" Ash shouted.

"It is mine, and mine alone!" Cyrus flung himself into the new universe. He disappeared into the swirling stars.

"Cyrus, sir! *Noooooooo!*" Mars lunged toward the universe, desperate to follow her leader. Saturn grabbed her and held tight.

Seconds later, the universe shrank in on itself and disappeared. It was gone.

So was Cyrus.

# CHAPTER 15

"**D**o you think everything will go back to normal now?" Dawn asked hopefully.

That was when Dialga and Palkia rose from where they had fallen. Wild and angry, they unleashed attack after attack, ripping holes in time and space.

Never before had so much energy been concentrated in one place. The effects were felt all across Sinnoh. Professor Rowan and his researchers had been monitoring the rising levels. Now they stared at their screens in alarm.

"The energy output from Mt. Coronet will surpass the critical point any second now!" the lead researcher reported.

"The energy that has surpassed the critical point is now rapidly inverting," Professor Rowan added.

"The entire Sinnoh region's energy is contracting toward Mt. Coronet!" the researcher said. "If it continues at this rate, Sinnoh will cease to exist!"

Dialga and Palkia's attacks had created a giant vortex, a tear in the fabric of space. It was too much energy for the universe to handle. And the tear was growing. Ash and his friends had to hold on tight so they didn't get sucked in!

"Is everyone all right?" Cynthia asked.

"Yeah!" they chorused. But if they didn't do something fast, they wouldn't be okay for long.

"I'm certain Dialga and Palkia haven't broken free yet," Cynthia said. "But if we aren't able to save them very soon, I'm afraid that energy mass will expand and engulf all of Sinnoh!"

The Lake Trio's eyes began to glow. They were trying to communicate again. Ash and his friends closed their eyes and concentrated.

"Combine our hearts as one," Dawn murmured, repeating what Mesprit told her.

"And please save Dialga and Palkia!" Brock recited his message from Mesprit.

Azelf told Ash the same thing.

"Let's go!" Ash said. "Okay, Azelf, do it!"

Azelf began to glow. Then, without hesitating, the Legendary Pokémon launched itself at the energy vortex. There was an enormous explosion, and the vortex disappeared.

"Azelf!" Ash cried, as the Pokémon dropped weakly into his arms. "Thank you!"

Dialga and Palkia were still thrashing wildly. Brock tried to soothe them. "Dialga! Palkia! The one who was tormenting you is gone. Please calm down."

But the Pokémon wouldn't — or couldn't — listen to him.

"You can do it," Brock promised Uxie. It floated toward Dialga and Palkia, trying to get them to stop.

But they were too angry. Which meant it was up to Mesprit. It unleashed an attack that covered the Pokémon in a dim green glow. When it faded away, Dialga and Palkia were finally calm.

The Lake Trio had done it!

The three Pokémon flew round and round in a circle, creating a glowing ring of energy. Dialga and Palkia floated into its center and disappeared.

Back in Professor Rowan's lab, the scientists celebrated. "The contracting energy levels have completely ceased!" one reported.

Professor Rowan frowned. Sinnoh was safe — but what about his friends? "Let's go. It's off to Mt. Coronet!"

As Professor Rowan sped toward the mountain, Ash, Brock, and Dawn were saying good-bye to the Lake Trio. It was time for the Legendary Pokémon to return to their own dimension.

"So, Azelf, Uxie, and Mesprit, why in the world did you choose us?" Ash asked them.

"It certainly seems obvious to me," Cynthia

said. "Azelf, Uxie, and Mesprit could sense how much you care about Pokémon."

Ash was overjoyed at the thought. "You mean it? Really?"

The Legendary Pokémon nodded. Then it was time for them to go. Ash, Brock, and Dawn waved good-bye to their new friends as the Lake Trio floated away, disappearing into the darkness.

"I wonder if we'll ever see them again," Ash said. He would never forget them, especially Azelf. But he was glad the Legendary Pokémon were going home.

"No doubt!" Dawn said, confident. She still felt a connection to Mesprit, and she suspected she always would.

"Yeah!" Brock said, knowing Uxie would always have a place in his heart.

Soon Gary Oak and Professor Rowan had arrived to check on their friends. Gary collected the precious stolen orbs, promising to get them back to Professor Carolina safe and sound.

Ash, Dawn, Brock, and Cynthia rejoined Looker. He seemed concerned.

"Looker, what's wrong?" Brock asked.

"I was just wondering where Team Rocket might've run off to," Looker said.

He didn't have to wonder for long. The Team Rocket hot air balloon was floating overhead.

"We beat Team Galactic at their own game!" James shouted gleefully.

"Sure did!" Jessie agreed. "And now *this* old world is all ours!"

"Once the Boss gets wind of this, we'll get a wind*fall*, y'all!" Meowth crowed.

James laughed. "My kind of wind."

"Heave ho!" Jessie cried. "Let the wind blow."

"Team Rocket finishes win, place, *and* show!" they shouted together. Then they floated off in search of trouble.

Well, at least Team Galactic wouldn't be causing anyone trouble ever again. They were in the back of a police van, waiting to be taken away.

"What happened to Cyrus?" Jupiter asked.

"He got away by himself," Saturn said.

"He *did*?" Jupiter couldn't believe their leader had abandoned them.

"Which means it's the end for Team Galactic," Saturn admitted.

Ash and his friends watched the police van drive away, proud that they had helped foil Team Galactic for good.

Cynthia smiled warmly at them. "Because there is sadness, we cherish happiness," she said. "And because there is anger, kindness is born. Thank you all! Sinnoh is still here, because you protected it."

"Wait, you mean *us*?" Ash asked.

Brock gaped at his friends. "Did she just say we protected Sinnoh?"

"If that's true, then it's because we had Piplup, Mesprit, and everyone else helping out. Isn't that right, Piplup?" said Dawn.

The little Water-type Pokémon agreed.

Ash grinned at his friends and all their Pokémon. He was eager to set off in search of more adventures. Whatever they found, whatever challenges they faced, he was sure he and his friends would triumph. Because now he knew they could do anything — as long as they had each other.

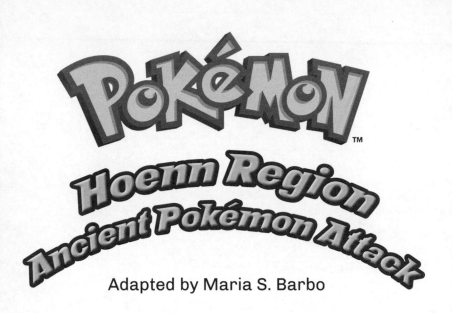

# POKÉMON™

## Hoenn Region
## Ancient Pokémon Attack

Adapted by Maria S. Barbo

Scholastic Inc.

# CHAPTER 1

"**T**hat was a big electrical attack," groaned ten-year-old Ash Ketchum. His red baseball cap covered his eyes.

Ash and his friends were floating on logs in the middle of the ocean. Team Rocket had just tried to steal Ash's Pikachu yet again. And failed *yet again*. But not before Pikachu had blasted them with a Thunderbolt that sent both sides flying in opposite directions!

Now, instead of sailing to Mossdeep City to battle a Gym Leader, Ash and his friends were stuck at sea.

*"Pi."* Pikachu rested its head on Ash's arm. The Electric-type Pokémon had no energy left.

"I'm turning into a giant prune!" May wailed.
May and her little brother, Max, had been
traveling with Ash throughout the Hoenn
region. May loved helping Pokémon get ready
for big contests. She was learning a lot about
them on this journey.

"Got any idea where we ended up, Brock?"
Max asked.

"I don't have a clue," said Brock. The former
Gym Leader had been traveling with Ash ever
since they'd battled each other in Pewter City.
Now Brock was studying to be a Pokémon doctor.

"Hopefully a ship will come by," Ash said. He raised his head to look around. Maybe a ship would magically appear just because he wanted it to!

Pikachu moaned in its sleep.

Suddenly, the friends were lifted up out of the water by what felt like a giant tidal wave.

Everyone screamed.

*"Pika?!"* shouted Pikachu, alarmed.

"What *is* this?" asked Ash.

"We're on top of a submarine," said Max.

"You're *kidding*," added May.

"That's great!" said Brock. "Ash, you just got what you were hoping for!"

"Cool!" Ash leaped to his feet. They were about to be rescued! He was already thinking about the food he'd eat as soon as they made it to Mossdeep City. "Now we just gotta let them know we're out here. Hey! Hey!" he shouted, and waved his arms.

*"Pika! PIKA!"* Pikachu jumped up and down.

"Can somebody help us?" May shouted. "Puh-*lease*!"

A boy wearing a red uniform and a hood with two black horns walked out onto the submarine's deck.

Ash and his friends quickly ducked down to hide.

"Team Magma," Ash muttered. "Not those guys!" Team Magma was made up of some of the biggest villains in the whole Hoenn region. They were always hunting for ancient Pokémon. Their rivals, Team Aqua, were just as bad.

The Team Magma member used a pair of binoculars to scan the horizon.

"What are the odds we'd end up on *their* submarine?" asked Brock.

"Of all the rotten luck," said May.

Pikachu pointed to a large red ship ahead. The submarine was heading straight for its cargo hold.

"Do you think that's Team Magma's secret base?" asked May.

*"Pika pika."* Pikachu was worried.

The large ship cast a shadow over the submarine, making it seem tiny and fragile. Ash and his friends stood as quiet as a Mr. Mime while the submarine slid into the base.

Through the ship's portholes, Ash could see a row of Team Magma members standing at attention inside. They were all wearing the same red uniform. Each one had their own snarling Mightyena by their side. In front of them stood an older man with slicked-back hair. He was definitely in charge.

"Reporting in, sir," said the boy from the deck. "The third division has completed its patrol."

"We'd better hide!" Ash said as Pikachu jumped onto his back.

"No kidding!" said May. "But where?" The friends all tried to scramble up the slippery metal wall of the submarine.

*"Grrrrrr."*

The friends froze. They could smell the rotten breath of a Mightyena right behind them.

There was no escaping now.

# CHAPTER 2

**A**sh and his friends held their arms in the air as the Mightyena marched them onto the ship.

"You needn't be so afraid," said the man in charge. "My name is Maxie. I'm the leader of Team Magma."

Pikachu and Ash gave Maxie the stink eye.

"Yeah?" said Ash. "So what are you going to do with us?" He felt his friends tense up beside him.

"Simmer down," said Maxie. "We're not going to hurt you."

"Huh?" Ash and his friends weren't sure they could trust this Maxie guy.

"It's just that we're a bit busy right now," Maxie said as he started walking. "So don't give us any trouble until our mission is complete."

"Mission?" asked May.

Ash and his friends followed Maxie to an office near the back of the ship.

"Please have a seat," Maxie said, pointing to a maroon couch. "I'm sure we can discuss this in a friendly way." But the Mightyena lining the room looked the opposite of friendly.

"Yeah, well," Ash said. "I'm not talking to you guys." Ash balled his hands into two fists. He always felt braver with Pikachu on his shoulder.

"Come on, Ash," said Brock. "I think we'd better hear what they have to say." Brock was a few years older than Ash and loved giving him advice.

"Yeah, why?" asked Ash.

*"Grrrrrrr,"* the Mightyena growled. May and Max screamed as the Dark-type Pokémon moved closer. Mightyena often sounded a deep growl before attacking.

"That's why," said Max. He was too young to have Pokémon of his own, but Max knew more about Pokémon than most Trainers.

Ash folded his arms across his chest and slowly sat down. Pikachu scowled at Maxie.

"Why am I getting the distinct feeling that you don't like us, Ash, hmm?" Maxie chuckled.

"'Cause I don't, that's why," said Ash. There was no way Team Magma's "mission" was going to be good for Pokémon.

"I know that you and Team Aqua aren't friends," said Ash. "But I also know that you want to steal ancient Pokémon and use them to do bad stuff." Ash jumped to his feet. Humans who tried to harm Pokémon made him so mad!

Three Mightyena stepped closer and snarled.

"Ash, calm down!" said Max. "I don't think you should be making them mad!" The younger boy clung to his sister.

"All I'm doing is telling the truth," Ash said.

"My friend, you are mistaken about us," said Maxie. He sat down behind a desk and folded his hands calmly. "Team Magma's sole purpose is to unravel the mysteries of our planet. In doing so, we will build a better world for everyone. We have absolutely nothing in common with a bunch of crooks like Team Aqua."

"Why should we trust you guys?" asked Ash.

"Either way," said Brock. "I'm sure you realize that ancient Pokémon are Legendary and not all that easy to capture."

"Of course," said Maxie, smiling. "But we already have our ancient Pokémon."

*"Pika?!"* asked Pikachu.

The friends gasped. Ancient Pokémon were very rare and *very* powerful.

This was getting worse and worse.

# CHAPTER 3

"That's right," Maxie told Ash and his friends. "Not only that, but we also have the ability to *control* ancient Pokémon." He took a blue glass ball out of the drawer and placed it calmly on the desk in front of him. "With this Blue Orb."

*"Pika?"* asked Pikachu. Ash leaned closer to get a better look.

Maxie was pleased by their surprise. He explained that long ago, there were a lot of storms and floods. The ancient Ground-type Pokémon Groudon wanted to help humans by making extra land for them to live on. So Groudon chased away the storm clouds and caused volcanoes to erupt. The lava from the volcanoes formed more land and the humans were happy.

"Our goal," Maxie told Ash, "is to use these Groudon in the very same way—to create more land. And to establish contact with their ancient world. You see, the power that world holds is way beyond measure." Maxie's voice grew grim. "But even as we speak, Team Aqua works against us. They seek to find Kyogre, whose powers oppose Groudon's."

Ash clenched his fists. Ancient Pokémon deserved to be respected. All this Maxie wanted was power. If Ash weren't surrounded by Team Magma, he'd show Maxie what Pikachu's electric attacks could do!

But Maxie didn't seem to notice Ash's anger.

"What Team Aqua does not know," Maxie continued, "is that we already have the Kyogre they seek!" He closed his eyes as if picturing the sleek, ancient Water-type Pokémon.

"You captured Kyogre, too?" asked Max. None of Ash's friends could believe what they were hearing.

"We thought perhaps it would help ruin Team Aqua's plans," said Maxie, grinning. "And then we discovered Team Aqua has a Groudon!"

Ash jumped up again. "That means both ancient Pokémon have been caught!" he shouted.

*"Pika?"* Pikachu's mouth opened wide.

"Regrettably," Maxie continued, "this Blue Orb can *only* control a Groudon. Team Aqua has a Red Orb—but a Red Orb can *only* control a Kyogre. The bottom line is that both of our groups are faced with holding a Pokémon that we are unable to control." He explained that they were meeting with Team Aqua on Monsu Island to swap Pokémon. "That's where we're heading now," he said proudly. Then his mood shifted. "But we can't have kids getting in our way. Tabitha, lock these children up at once!"

"Right," said a boy standing beside the desk.

Team Magma's Mightyena snarled and circled Ash and his friends.

"Hey, you can't—" Ash was ready to fight, but a loud siren made everyone stop.

"Malfunction in Kyogre's cargo hold!" said a voice over a loudspeaker.

Was the ancient Water-type Pokémon trying to escape?

# CHAPTER 4

**D**eep inside the ship, a Legendary Pokémon opened its eyes.

While Ash and his friends had been speaking with Maxie, a girl in a Team Magma uniform crept out of the submarine. She walked confidently down a long, shiny corridor. She knew exactly where she was headed.

The girl found two Team Magma guards standing outside a set of sliding metal doors. They were holding long sticks, but she wasn't scared.

"Everything under control?" she asked them.

The guards stood up straighter.

"Yes, ma'am," they answered.

"That's good," the girl said quietly. Then she knocked out the guards with a one-two punch.

She pulled down her hood to reveal a long swath of red hair. "I knew I could count on you."

Without wasting any time, the girl used one of the guards' security passes to open the door to a large science lab. A Water-type Pokémon the size of a submarine was trapped in a tank filled with water. It was being held down by large metal cuffs.

"You'll be free very soon, Kyogre," the girl said to it with a devious smile. She quickly found a control panel and punched in the code: 00314. A red bar lit up at the top of the screen, and the doors to Kyogre's prison opened.

The enormous Sea Basin Pokémon growled and pushed against its restraints.

"Yes!" shouted the red-haired girl. She pumped a fist in the air. "Let's go, Kyogre, now!"

With a powerful roar, Kyogre broke free of the metal cuffs and burst out of its tank. It crashed right through the side of the ship and dove deep into the ocean. The whole boat tipped sideways, and the humans inside screamed.

Kyogre was finally free!

Back inside the ship, the girl quickly headed up to the deck. Smoke billowed around her. "This is Shelly," she said into her headset. "The plan's a success."

"Bravo," said a voice behind her.

Shelly turned around, startled. A strange boy dressed like a member of Team Magma stood watching her. But a real rival would have already tried to capture her.

"I wouldn't expect anything less from the strategic commander for Team Aqua," the boy continued. "Nice disguise."

Shelly scowled at him and then a smile crossed her face.

"Thanks," she told him as she crossed her arms. "You're not exactly a Team Magma member yourself."

"I'm only here to help," said the stranger. "I realize how important it is to release Kyogre to the sea. How else can it be controlled by the Red Orb?"

"That's right," said Shelly. She didn't know who this boy was or why he was familiar with

Team Aqua's plan—and she didn't care. Before
he could keep talking, she pulled off her red
Team Magma disguise to reveal a sleek blue-
and-gray Team Aqua wet suit.

"And very soon Team Aqua will have the
power to rule the world!" she shouted. Without
waiting for his reply, she did a backflip over the
ship's railing and dove into the sea.

The boy scrunched up his eyebrows but
stayed calm.

"Don't count on it," he said as he watched her
swim away. "You may be powerful, Team Aqua,
but so am I."

# CHAPTER 5

**B**ack in Maxie's office, Ash and his friends screamed as the ship lurched sideways.

"What was that?" asked Ash as sirens blared all over the ship.

"Fire in the engine room!" said a voice over the loudspeaker. "Damage to the port side! We're sinking!"

The Team Magma members who had lined the wall jumped into action.

Maxie banged his fists on his desk and stood up. He had come too far in his plan to end up losing Kyogre now. "Seal up the seventh and eighth bulkheads immediately!" he commanded. "Call the security force and—"

An explosion behind Maxie knocked him forward. The Blue Orb flew into the air.

"Get it, Ash!" Brock shouted.

Ash nodded. This was his chance to save the world by ruining Team Magma's plan.

"Pikachu!" he called. "Let's go!"

*"Pi . . ."* Pikachu bent its knees. *"Kaaa . . ."* It pushed off the ground. *"Chu!"* Pikachu cried as it sprang into the air.

"No you don't," shouted Tabitha. "Mightyena, now!"

Three snarling Bite Pokémon leaped into the air to challenge Pikachu.

"Don't give in, Pikachu!" called Ash.

But Pikachu never gave in.

*"Pi. Ka . . . !"*

The yellow Electric-type Pokémon jumped onto the first Mightyena's forehead and used it as a springboard to leap onto the next Mightyena's head. Pikachu bounced from one to the other until it was within inches of the Blue Orb.

*"Chuuu!"* With one final push, Pikachu wrapped its arms around the orb. The Pokémon did two somersaults and landed on its feet. Maxie and Tabitha watched in shock.

"You did it, Pikachu!" Ash pumped a fist.

Maxie growled. The orb began to glow in Pikachu's arms.

*"Pika?"*

"Whoa!" said Ash. He and his friends watched as the orb started to blink. A strange red pattern flashed on its surface. It looked like a circle with three even lines coming out of the top.

"Get that orb back!" Maxie shouted. But his team didn't move. Something was happening. The orb glowed, shrank down to the size of a Poké Ball, and was absorbed into Pikachu's body.

Pikachu fell back in surprise.

"Pikachu?" Ash reached for his Pokémon.

"I want that Pikachu *now*!" shouted Maxie.

Tabitha was dazed but quickly recovered.

"Go, Mightyena!" he commanded. The pack of Dark-type Pokémon snarled and leaped at Pikachu.

But a force field of electricity was already radiating off Pikachu's body. Its eyes glowed red, and the strange circular pattern from the Blue Orb spread onto Pikachu's forehead. Sparks flew from its cheeks.

*"PikaCHUUUUU!"* Pikachu cried as it blasted the three Mightyena into Maxie and Tabitha. The force knocked Team Magma to the ground and sent Pikachu flying back into Ash's arms.

"Hold on," said Max, shocked. "Was that a Thunderbolt?"

"It was," answered Brock, "but much more powerful."

"And what's that weird pattern that keeps showing up?" asked May.

Pikachu seemed to be battling a strong force inside its own body. The yellow Pokémon

was shaking as the pattern from the Blue Orb flashed onto its belly.

"Pikachu!" Ash cried. He cradled his limp Pokémon in his arms.

"Now's our chance to get out of here!" called Brock.

Ash and his friends ran as Maxie and Tabitha slowly rose to their feet.

"Are you all right, sir?" asked Tabitha.

"I'm fine," said Maxie. "But you've *got* to hurry it up and capture that Pikachu!"

# CHAPTER 6

"**A**rchie, sir!" shouted Shelly.

Far out at sea, a blue-gray submarine emerged from the water. Shelly stood on the deck with Archie, the leader of Team Aqua. She looked more like a pirate now that she was wearing her own uniform—a bandana tied around her head, a crop top, and baggy pants. "We have successfully released Kyogre from Team Magma's ship according to plan!" She had to shout to be heard above the sound of the crashing waves and the din of the submarine's engines.

"Excellent work, Shelly," said Archie. "You have once again proven yourself worthy of my trust." Archie pulled the Red Orb out of his black jumpsuit. "So now I think we should get this show on the road . . ."

The orb began to glow.

"Convey our will to Kyogre, great Red Orb!" Archie shouted. Shelly watched with a smile on her face. "Allow this great power to be released now!" Bands of red light shot from the orb out into the sky and water. Archie tightened his grip.

Deep at the bottom of the ocean, Kyogre heard the call. It burst up through the surface emblazoned with an ancient blue pattern similar to the one on Pikachu. Kyogre hovered above the water and roared. It was ready.

Legend says that Kyogre is the sea in Pokémon form. When it channels the full power of nature, Kyogre can raise sea levels with mighty storms.

"Kyogre, together, you and I can make quite a team!" Archie shouted. "It's time to finish this up once and for all!"

A burst of energy shot from the ancient Pokémon's mouth and delivered the final blow to Team Magma's submarine.

\*    \*    \*

Back on the deck of Team Magma's sinking sub, the boy who'd found Shelly was ready and waiting for the attack.

"Dragonite, you and I must stop Kyogre's wrath," he said to the Poké Ball in his hand. "But I'm afraid we'll need some help—"

"No!" a girl's voice interrupted his thoughts. "We can't dive in the ocean from *here*!" May screamed.

The boy looked down over the railing. Ash and his friends were huddled up on the deck below, trying to work up enough courage to jump.

"Yeah, I'm scared!" cried Max. He looked down at the choppy waves, and his face turned the same green color as his hair.

"But we've *gotta* jump," Ash said. "There's no choice!"

The mysterious boy sucked in a breath.

"It's Ash!" he said out loud. "What's *he* doing here?" The boy, whose name was Lance, had helped Ash fight Team Rocket back at the Lake of Rage. Lance was worried for the young Pokémon Trainers, but part of him was also relieved. Ash, Brock, and May were excellent with Pokémon. They had a strong sense of justice. They just might be the help he needed. But at the moment, they were still trying to get off the sinking ship.

"All right, guys," Lance heard Brock call out. "Just close your eyes and *jump!*" Lance watched as Brock, May, and Max gripped the railing. But before they could dive, another explosion sent them flying over the edge. The friends screamed as they fell into the raging waves.

Ash ran to the railing, holding Pikachu tightly.

"Pikachu!" Ash shouted. "We're going in . . ."

*Crrr—aaack!*

There was a loud explosion, and Ash's feet

flew out from under him. He gripped Pikachu as they fell to the ground. When Ash looked up, they were completely surrounded by Tabitha and his pack of snarling Mightyena.

"Foolish child," said Tabitha with a smirk. "You weren't planning on going anywhere, were you?"

Ash looked around for an escape, but there was no way to get around the drooling Bite Pokémon. And Pikachu was still too weak to help him.

"Maxie is already on the plane for Monsu Island," Tabitha told Ash. "And we must go there immediately. Now, be a good little boy, and come with me." The Mightyena marched Ash up a gangplank toward a small red plane.

*Monsu Island*, Lance noted. He watched as Brock, May, and Max bobbed in the water below. He may not be able to help *Ash* right now. But his mission wasn't over yet.

# CHAPTER 7

"That's what you call a blastoff," Jessie groaned.

Jessie, James, and Meowth lay on their backs in the sand. They were still reeling from Pikachu's surprise electric attack earlier that morning. All they'd wanted was to bring Pikachu back to the Boss, but those twerps had sent them blasting off again!

Meowth spit sand out of his mouth. He could hear waves lapping against the shore, but it only made his head hurt more.

James clutched his stomach. "Any idea where we are?" he asked. He opened his eyes slightly to look around.

"Some deserted island somewhere?" Meowth groaned. He heard the double propellers of a

plane flying overhead. "Hmm?" He opened his eyes wide.

"Isn't that Team Magma hovering past?" James asked. A red plane flew over a cliff and out of their view.

Jessie slowly sat up.

"So much for the *deserted island* theory," she said, brushing the sand off her uniform.

Meowth leaped to his feet. "Let's GO!" he shouted at the rest of Team Rocket. "Now it's a *somethin's up* theory!" He shook his paw at Jessie and James to get them moving.

Wobbuffet popped up out of nowhere to support Meowth.

*"WOBBUFFET!"* the blue Psychic-type Pokémon shouted.

Jessie and James followed Meowth to the top of a cliff. They heard voices and ducked down behind some bushes. A large force of Team Aqua members had gathered to greet Team Magma's plane. Team Rocket recognized two of the people as Archie and Shelly, the leaders of Team Aqua.

Archie chuckled as the head of Team Magma walked off the plane followed by part of his

team and their Mightyena. Archie clearly thought he had the upper hand in whatever was about to go down.

"How are you, Maxie?" Team Rocket heard Archie ask.

The two rivals stared each other down.

"You have insulted the name of Team Magma!" Maxie snarled.

Archie smiled.

"Nah!" he said, tilting his head to the side. "But *these* two might have!" Behind him, two Team Aqua prisoners were tied up with rope.

"Now if I'm not mistaken," said Archie, "one of these two men is your commander, correct? I would assume his mission was to steal our Groudon, although he failed quite miserably, didn't he?!"

The two prisoners struggled against their binds.

Maxie gritted his teeth in anger.

Jessie, James, and Meowth poked their heads up from behind the bushes.

"They have prisoners!" Jessie squealed. She clapped her hands together.

"This is good," said James with a gleeful smile. "Let's stay and see what happens."

Jessie and James watched as Archie and Maxie argued.

"First you call for a meeting and then you try and sabotage us?" Archie asked. He opened his arms wide and then stuck his hands in his pockets. "That's not exactly the best way to do business."

Maxie took a step closer. Team Rocket leaned forward. Maybe there would be a fight!

"Look, Archie, you know as well as I do that the Groudon means absolutely *nothing* to you or your organization!" Maxie said. He was tense. "So why don't you hand it over?"

Archie threw his head back and laughed.

"I guess you just don't realize what a predicament you're in!" he said. Suddenly, his face was serious. "Fact is, we've got *Kyogre*, too!"

"You *what*?" Maxie clearly wasn't expecting this twist.

Archie stood with his hands on his hips. "Here's the deal," he said, ready to set the

terms. "Team Magma will break up *today* while Team Aqua will rule the world."

Maxie clenched his teeth, but Archie was enjoying the moment.

"Or, if you prefer, I could use Kyogre to destroy everything while you stand there," Archie said. He calmly reached back into his jumpsuit and pulled out the Red Orb. The two men growled at each other as Team Rocket watched from the hillside.

"This is better than my favorite soap opera," James said.

But Jessie was still trying to get the story

straight. "So Team Aqua managed to capture *both* Pokémon and now wants Team Magma to break *up*?" she asked.

Meowth raised a paw into the air. "Well, *I* always say, when ya got a bunch of crooks tryin' to out-crook one another, THAT'S the time when ya swoop in on 'em!"

James wasn't catching on.

"Wow," he said. "You think Team Aqua really thinks it can rule the world?"

"They *do* have two ancient Pokémon on their side," Jessie said thoughtfully.

*"No!"* shouted Meowth. He jumped up and down. Why did they never understand? *"We're* gonna go steal 'em, and then give 'em to the Boss as a gift!"

*"Oh!"* said Jessie and James. "Yay!"

All three members of Team Rocket began pumping their arms in the air with glee. "Let's go put our promotion into motion!" they shouted.

*"Wobba!"* agreed Wobbuffet. *"WOBBUFFET!"*

# CHAPTER 8

"*P ika? Pika!*" said Pikachu.

Ash held his Pokémon in his arms as it slept fitfully. Tabitha had locked them up in the cargo hold of the plane Team Magma had flown to Monsu Island.

"It'll be okay, Pikachu," said Ash, but he wasn't so sure. "Hang in there, buddy."

"*Pika! Pika!*" Pikachu's eyes narrowed and began to glow red. The strange ancient pattern appeared all over its body. Pikachu wriggled in Ash's arms. Thunderbolts shot out of Pikachu's cheeks.

"Pikachu!" cried Ash as his Pokémon burst out of his arms.

"*Pika, pikachuuuuuuuuu!*" it cried as it released a Thunderbolt almost as big as the

one in Maxie's office. Pikachu blasted a hole in the ceiling and shattered the nearby storage crates.

Ash covered his face with his arms as pieces of the ceiling crumbled around him. Smoke filled the crowded space.

*"PIKA!"* Pikachu shouted, radiating electric energy. *"PIKA!"*

Then Pikachu staggered. The red pattern blinked on and off. Pikachu wobbled as if dizzy.

*"Pika . . ."* the Electric-type Pokémon said before falling forward onto its face. *"Chuuu!"*

"Pikachu!" Ash jumped to his feet and scooped up his Pokémon. "I don't understand what's wrong."

Just then, the door to the cargo hold opened. Ash pulled Pikachu close to his chest. A member of Team Magma strode through the door.

"Back off!" Ash cried. "No *way* are you getting Pikachu from me!"

"Hey, Ash!" called the intruder. He pulled down his hood to reveal a head of spiky red hair. "It's *me*, Lance!"

Ash's whole face brightened. "Lance, no WAY!" he shouted. Lance was a Pokémon Champion, a member of the Elite Four, *and* part of the Pokémon G-Men. Their mission was to stop people who mistreated Pokémon. Ash had helped Lance fight Team Rocket and catch a red Gyarados!

*"Shhh . . . !"* Lance raised a finger to his lips. He looked back over his shoulder to make sure no one had followed him. "I'm undercover doing research. My assignment was to stop Team

Aqua and Team Magma from misusing ancient Pokémon!"

"*That's* what they're doing?" Ash asked. But he didn't have time to worry about their evil plans. "Something happened to Pikachu!"

"Yes," said Lance. "Your Pikachu bonded with that Blue Orb, didn't it?" Lance explained that the intense energy inside the Blue and Red Orbs could control ancient Pokémon—and *any* living being who came in contact with them for too long.

"Oh no!" Ash shouted.

"You know," said Lance, "even humans have to be *extremely* careful when they're handling

the orbs." Lance knelt down in front of Ash and Pikachu. "Since your Pikachu is such a small Pokémon, it was unable to resist the energy of the orb."

"*Pi*," groaned Pikachu. Its cheeks were blinking red. "*Pi.*"

Ash scrunched his eyebrows. He was worried.

"So then Lance—what do you think is gonna happen to Pikachu?" Ash asked.

"Don't worry!" said Lance. He placed a hand on Ash's shoulder. "I promise you, I'll find a way to break Pikachu's bond with the Blue Orb. Now you two just wait here a little bit longer, okay?"

Ash nodded and tried to stay calm. But as soon as Lance left the cargo hold, Pikachu's body shook with electric power. Ash wrapped his arms around his Pokémon pal to keep it grounded, but the electricity coming off Pikachu made that impossible. Pikachu cried out in pain.

"Pikachu!" Ash shouted. "You're gonna be okay!"

# CHAPTER 9

"There it is!" said Jessie. She pointed at a blue submarine floating just offshore.

"It's a submarine full of Team Aqua guys!" said Meowth.

"That's not *all* it's full of," said James, with a thrill in his voice. "It's loaded down with that Kyogre and Groudon, too!"

"Shall we lighten their load?" Jessie asked.

All three members of Team Rocket pumped their fists in the air.

Wobbuffet popped up to show its team spirit. *"WOB-BUH, WOB-BUH, BUFFET!"* shouted the Patient Pokémon.

Team Rocket slunk down the cliff to get closer to the submarine.

"Okay," said Jessie. "Let's get a move on and grab that Pokémon before they get back."

Team Rocket tiptoed over to a computer screen where they could watch Kyogre. The ancient Pokémon was as big as a ship and floated in a small rectangular tank.

"That Kyogre sure can fill a tub!" said Meowth.

"I hope we have a good plan," said James.

"Of *course* we do," said Jessie. She pulled out a giant net launcher and rested it on her shoulder.

Meowth cheered. "One net comin' up!" He began randomly pressing buttons on the computer's keyboard, but nothing happened.

"Uhhhhhh, hello?" he said.

James shoved Meowth aside.

"Let a *real* button pusher show you how it's done!" he shouted.

Meowth side-kicked James in the chest.

James's jaw dropped. "Now you're pushin' *my* buttons!" he said.

"Maybe it needs a little finesse," Jessie suggested.

"All right, then, how's *this* for finesse?!" said Meowth. He started pounding on the buttons until the computer made a *womp-womp* noise. The screen went blank.

"Oops," said Meowth.

"Now you've broken it, Meowth," Jessie scolded.

Meowth raised a paw and turned to face her.

"If you and James woulda just butted out, it woulda worked *fine!*" he yelled.

"*WOB-BUH!*" Wobbuffet slammed a flipper down on one of the large rectangular computer keys.

There was an explosion and a puff of smoke.

And then the door to Kyogre's tank slid right open.

Team Rocket did a happy dance.

"And we're off!" said Jessie.

*"Wobbuffet!"* said Wobbuffet.

"Time to go claim our prize!" said James.

Team Rocket ran inside the submarine— and crashed right into two members of Team Aqua!

"Are you from Team Magma?" the boy member of Team Aqua asked.

Team Rocket ignored him and tried to keep walking, but the Team Aqua's Crawdaunt blocked their path.

*"Crawdaunt!"* the Water- and Dark-type Pokémon shouted.

"And where do you think *you're* going?" the girl member of Team Aqua asked.

Jessie nodded at James and Meowth. "Let's get what we came for!" she shouted.

James pulled out a Poké Ball.

"Ready!" he said. "Cacnea! Pin Missile!" James threw the Poké Ball forward to release a green Grass-type Pokémon.

*"Cacnea! Cacne-ne-ne-nea!"* the Cactus Pokémon shouted as it blasted Team Aqua and their Crawdaunt with a shower of pin needles.

Team Aqua screamed and passed out.

Jessie and James didn't waste any time. Quickly, they ran toward Kyogre's tank.

"It's time to come with *us* now, Kyogre!" said Jessie. She raised her net launcher and shot it at Kyogre. A large net covered the Pokémon's whole body.

"Now, seal the deal with an electric attack!" Jessie said as she pressed a button. The net crackled with electricity.

"You might be an old-fogy Pokémon, but you're *still* a Water-type!" said James as he raised a fist in glee. He knew that Water-type Pokémon were weak against Electric-type Pokémon.

"Which means there's no fightin' back!" Meowth chimed in.

But the ancient Pokémon hadn't existed for centuries without learning a trick or two. With a giant roar, it rocketed up out of the tank and broke through the net. Kyogre tossed the

electrified net on top of Team Rocket and then dove back into the ocean. It was free again!

"Huh?" asked Meowth. He wasn't expecting this.

As the net landed on Team Rocket, it suddenly shocked them, and they screamed. The force of the electric charge blew off the top of the submarine.

"We're blasting off again?!" cried Team Rocket as they flew off into the sky.

# CHAPTER 10

"**A**rchie, sir!" Shelly ran to where her team leader stood in front of a gray stone pyramid. "I have word that Kyogre has been released to the sea!" she said.

"Just as I planned . . ." Archie said with a slight smile. He pulled the Red Orb out of his jumpsuit and walked over to Team Magma.

"Maxie!" he said dramatically. "I invite you to witness as Team Aqua claims the world for its own!"

Without waiting for a response, Archie started climbing the stone pyramid. A small blue hovercraft was waiting for him at the top.

"Please!" Maxie shouted. He ran toward the stone steps. "Don't do it!"

But Shelly was ready to protect her team leader. She wasn't going to let anything stop Team Aqua's plan now that it was in motion.

"Prepare to give Archie protection!" she called to her teammates.

Several members of Team Aqua stepped forward.

"Right!" they said.

Shelly reached for a Poké Ball.

"Walrein! I choose you!" she shouted. Her teammates did the same.

Three Walrein burst from their Poké Balls.

"Water Gun, NOW!" Shelly commanded.

The Ice Break Pokémon sprang into action. They sprayed Maxie and his team with powerful blasts of ice-cold water.

Maxie covered his face with his arm as Tabitha took charge.

"Go, Mightyena!" Tabitha commanded. "It's time to fight back!" Three snarling Mightyena flew out of their Poké Balls.

"Shadow Ball, let's go!" called Tabitha.

The Mightyena didn't miss a beat. They breathed black balls of energy at their watery opponents.

But the Walrein's Water Gun attack knocked out the Mightyena before they could land their move.

Both teams could hear Archie laughing from the top of the pyramid.

"Kyogre," he called as he stepped onto the hovercraft. "The world awaits!"

Deep in the ocean, Kyogre heard the powerful call of the Red Orb. The Pokémon shot up from the waves and roared.

"That's right, Maxie, I'm up here!" Archie taunted.

"Go, sir!" Tabitha said to an angry Maxie. "You *must* pursue him! We'll handle things back here!"

Maxie clenched his teeth and strode toward his plane. Someone had to take down Archie. And he was determined to do it.

# CHAPTER 11

"**A**aaaah!" A giant wave smashed against the cliff ledge where Team Rocket clung to one another in fear. Meowth scrambled up into Jessie's lap.

"Of all the nice places we could've landed, we end up . . . *here?*" Jessie said. Her voice was shaking.

"Can't we blast off to a *happy* place?" James whined.

"Well, *I'm* happy . . ." said Meowth. His entire body trembled in fear. "To be ALIVE!"

*"WOOOOO-BUH!"* agreed Wobbuffet.

From their perch, Team Rocket could just make out Archie as he hovered above the pyramid. The wind carried his voice to the cliff.

"And now, observe this power," said Archie in a commanding tone. He held the orb high above his head and cried out to the ancient Sea Basin Pokémon. "Kyogre! Sink the land into the sea!"

The orb glowed, and the blue pattern shone on Kyogre's body.

The great Pokémon sliced through the surface of the water toward Archie. It roared and drew lightning and thunder down from the clouds. Rain pounded the ocean. The storm made the water swirl into dangerous riptides. Kyogre soared into the air.

Team Rocket gripped one another as the rain poured down on them. Lightning cracked nearby, and the waves nearly wiped them off the cliffside. They all closed their eyes and screamed.

"We could use some *help* here!" Jessie called into the air.

"Come on, Meowth, *do* something!" pleaded James.

"I *am*," answered Meowth. "I'm freakin' out!"

\*   \*   \*

Meanwhile, Maxie watched in outrage as the storm gained force. There was no way his plane could take off in this wind.

Archie laughed from high above.

"Oh well, Maxie," he called to his foe. "I was hoping that you'd be able to witness my conquest of the world. Now it doesn't look like that will be possible, sadly. But *this* should give you a taste. That island you're on will soon be swallowed up by the sea!" Archie's eyes glowed with rage.

"Archie, are you *out of your mind*?" Maxie called. He tried to reason with his opponent.

"There are people on this island, as well as your *own*!" Would he really abandon his own team?

Archie narrowed his eyes and tightened his grip on the orb.

"So what?" he laughed.

Shelly gasped. That wasn't like Archie.

"But, Archie, what do you mean?!" she cried out. They always had each other's backs. And leaving her to drown as Monsu Island sank into the sea had never been part of their plan.

Lance knew it was time to step in and reveal his true identity to Maxie and Archie. He pulled down his red hood and stepped forward. Maybe Archie would be impressed by the legendary power of the G-Men and stand down.

"Listen, Archie!" called Lance. "You must release the Red Orb or you will become *obsessed* by it!"

"I don't *think* so," Archie said, sounding almost bored. He turned toward the sea and once again held the glowing Red Orb above his head.

"Let's go, Kyogre!" he called.

Kyogre beat its fins together and let out a fierce roar.

A tower of light shot down from the storm clouds. The ancient Pokémon's power knocked out Team Aqua's Walrein and Team Magma's Mightyena.

"Hurry," Shelly called to her team, "gather up all the Pokémon!"

"Round up the Mightyena quickly!" Tabitha commanded Team Magma.

Despite the earth-shattering thunder, they could still hear Archie's crazed laughter.

Lance would not give up. He had to make Archie and Maxie understand what was happening.

"That Red Orb was created by evil people long ago to control ancient Pokémon and then

use them as weapons!" Lance told them. "But the ancient power of the Pokémon was much, much greater. As the ancient Pokémon became more evil, the people who *controlled* them also became more evil! This is why the two orbs were sealed away: to keep humans from making the same mistakes!"

"No!" said Maxie. He would not believe it. His team had been studying the orbs for years. He was sure only *weak* people could be controlled by them. "We *need* those ancient Pokémon! They're necessary for us to build a better world for everyone!"

"How can you believe such nonsense?" Lance snapped.

At that moment, a bolt of lightning shattered the ground between Lance and Maxie.

Archie raised the orb, and Kyogre responded by turning the storm clouds into tornadoes and the ocean waves into whirlpools. A tidal wave rose up out of the sea and headed for the island.

"Quickly!" Shelly shouted. "All hands into the ruins!"

# CHAPTER 12

**B**ack inside Team Magma's plane, a sudden blast knocked Ash over.

*"Pi. Pika,"* said Pikachu weakly. Then it fell from Ash's arms onto the cold, slick ground.

"Pikachu!" Ash called out. "Pikachu?"

But Pikachu was answering another call. Its eyes glowed red as the power of the Blue Orb once again surged through its body. The ancient red pattern blazed across its yellow fur.

"Pikachu!" Ash cried. "No!" But there was nothing Ash could do.

Pikachu rose up and roared, baring its sharp teeth. It blasted the wall with electricity until the wall split open.

Then Pikachu slipped out of the cargo hold and into the raging storm.

"Pikachu, come back!" Ash called. He tried to run after Pikachu, but the gash in the wall was too narrow.

Before he could panic, Ash heard friendly voices calling his name.

"Huh?" Ash said. *Brock? May? Max?* "Hey, you guys!" His friends were okay! And they were here just when he needed them most!

"Hey, Ash!" Brock called. "We're out here with Lance! Lance sent his red Gyarados to fish us out of the sea and bring us safely to Monsu Island."

"Hey, Lance!" Ash jumped to his feet. "Pikachu just ran out through this hole!"

"Oh no!" said May.

"I need to get outta here and look for Pikachu!" Ash cried. But before he could move, he felt a terrible wind.

*"TIDAL WAVE!"* Max shouted. He grabbed his sister's hand. Off the shore, a wall of water was quickly making its way toward the tiny island.

"We'd better move, guys!" said Brock, trying to stay calm for his friends.

"Stand back," Lance told Ash. "Dragonite can help you get out."

Ash stepped away from the opening as Lance hurled a Poké Ball into the air.

"Dragonite!" Lance called. "Come out and use Dragon Claw!"

The kindhearted Dragon Pokémon burst from its Poké Ball with a roar. Its claws were already glowing with power. With a mighty slash, Dragonite freed Ash from the cargo hold.

"That was great, Lance. Thanks!" said Ash. The friends quickly made a plan. Lance and Dragonite would go take care of Archie and get the Red Orb back. Meanwhile, Ash and his friends would go find Pikachu.

Lance climbed onto Dragonite and flew into the stormy sky as Ash and his friends ran into the woods. But the friends were not alone. Tabitha was hot on their trail, and under Maxie's orders, he wasn't letting them out of his sight.

Lance and Dragonite sped toward Kyogre. They watched Archie land his hovercraft on the ancient Pokémon's brow.

"Bwah, ha, ha, ha!" Archie laughed. "Do your worst, Kyogre!" He clutched the Red Orb tightly in his palm. "Your *worst*, I say!"

Dragonite swooped closer, fighting against the storm.

"Archie!" Lance called. "Give up the Red Orb at *once*!" The wind blew back his red flame of hair.

"Not on your life," Archie cackled. "Kyogre, get 'em!"

Kyogre rocketed up into the sky. It used Aqua Ring to spew a powerful tunnel of water at Lance and Dragonite.

"Dodge it!" Lance called to his Pokémon.

Dragonite just barely ducked out of the way in time. Somehow, Lance managed not to fall off—but he knew he needed backup.

"Now, Gyarados!" he called. "Hyper Beam!" His red Pokémon soared into the air to meet Kyogre

head-on. Gyarados formed a glowing ball of energy in its mouth and then spat it at Kyogre.

Archie didn't miss a beat. "Now for a REAL Hyper Beam!" he called to Kyogre.

Kyogre roared and shot a Hyper Beam of its own that met Gyarados's midway. The two beams canceled each other out. There was a massive explosion.

"There is no one in the *world* who can stop me now!" Archie growled. "And soon, this whole world will be all *mine*!" As he spoke, the Red Orb glowed with the ancient blue pattern. It melted into Archie's hands, sending a shock wave of power coursing through his body. With his arms

outstretched, Archie leaned his head back and howled.

"They bonded!" said Lance, half in disbelief. But Archie only laughed as the glowing blue pattern blinked onto his chest. His eyes glowed blue with power.

# CHAPTER 14

"**A**AAAAAH!" Team Rocket screamed in panic. A giant wave and a blue submarine were coming right at them! The submarine crashed onshore inches from Meowth's head.

"Wake me up when it's over," the Scratch Cat Pokémon groaned. Rain pelted his face.

"Whaddaya say we get outta here while we can?" James suggested.

"Are you nuts?" Jessie snapped. "We can't emerge from a life-or-death situation empty-handed!" She looked up at Team Aqua's submarine. "There's still a *Groudon* left, you know!"

"Leftovers?" Meowth asked. Now this sounded good!

*"WO-bbuffet!"* Wobbuffet chimed in. It was the deciding vote. They would check out the submarine and steal the ancient Continent Pokémon for the Boss!

Team Rocket scrambled toward the submarine and quickly found Groudon's cell. A computer screen showed the ancient Pokémon standing beneath a metal arch with its arms and legs cuffed.

"Well, there it is," said James. "But it's locked inside."

"Then get it out!" commanded Jessie.

"But what if Groudon cops a Kyogre-esque attitude?" asked James. After everything they had been through, he was a little frightened.

"Worry not!" said Meowth, raising a paw. "I got the perfect plan! First, we go and attack Kyogre and make it really mad. Then it'll whip up one of those super tsunamis, which we grab a ride on with the submarine." Meowth paused to take a deep breath. "And *then* we're outta here, with both the submarine *and* the Groudon!"

Jessie and James thought about it for a second.

"I suppose it's possible . . ." said James. He rubbed his chin.

"It's sheer *brilliance*!" said Jessie, clapping her hands.

"Thanks!" said Meowth. "*I* thought so!"

*Crrr—aaack!* A giant Thunderbolt shocked Team Rocket. They screamed.

"No, *that* was brilliance," James groaned.

Team Rocket looked up to see who had shocked them.

Pikachu stood on a nearby ledge with its arms outstretched and its eyes glowing red. Its bright cheeks sparked with electric energy.

*"PI-KA!"* Pikachu roared, showing off its sharp, pointy teeth.

"Ain't that *Pikachu*?" Meowth asked, eyes wide.

"I *think* so . . ." said James. The Pikachu they knew had always looked so chipper, like such a goody-goody. But this Pikachu had a strange red pattern on its body and looked almost evil.

"I guess we're seeing a whole new side," said Jessie. She kind of liked it.

They watched as that twerp Ash and his friends ran up behind Pikachu. But they were too late. The Mouse Pokémon jumped down onto the shipping container that held Groudon.

"PIKACHU!" shouted Pikachu, charging up its electric power and sending bolts of lightning into the dark sky.

Team Rocket saw Maxie and Tabitha run out onto another nearby ledge.

"What's that Pikachu doing?" asked Maxie.

"That's *quite* an Electric attack!" Meowth said.

"Coming from *our* little Pikachu!" James said, proudly.

"It's not ours yet, but it's gonna be!" said Jessie. James pulled out their net blaster. Meowth bounced from paw to paw in a happy dance.

"Show me that cute face!" James shouted to Pikachu. He moved the net blaster until he had Pikachu in its sights.

Pikachu locked eyes with James.

*"Pika? Pi-KA!"* shouted Pikachu, and it sent the full power of its Thunderbolt flying at Team Rocket!

The electric shock shook their bodies and lifted them off the ground.

"Why'd you have to let it know we were here?" Jessie asked.

"Because it just didn't seem right to take it from behind," said James.

"Just another *brilliant* idea!" Meowth yelled as they blasted off *again*.

# CHAPTER 15

"*PIKA!*" Pikachu drew lightning down out of the sky.

A crowd of Team Aqua and Team Magma members gathered below. Ash and his friends watched from the rock ledge.

"No, Pikachu!" Ash shouted. He knew his Pokémon well enough to understand what was about to happen. "Pikachu, please STOP!"

The sky turned purple as Pikachu channeled the electric current of the storm into a funnel of electricity—and blasted the roof off Groudon's cell.

Lance and Dragonite zoomed in closer to get a better view.

"How can this be *possible*?" Lance wondered.

"What's happening?" cried May.

Inside the submarine, the ancient Ground-type Pokémon was waking up from a long sleep.

Archie laughed from his perch on the hovercraft. This was the moment he'd been waiting for. Now that Groudon was free, he could use Kyogre to defeat it. Then Archie would take the Blue Orb and rule the whole world—the sea *and* the land!

Archie's chest glowed with the ancient blue pattern. Kyogre slowly rose up from beneath the water, ready for Archie's next command.

*"Pika!"* Pikachu cried as Groudon's cell burst open. Smoke and flames rose up around them.

Ash reached for his Pokémon. "Pikachu!" he shouted. "No!"

The ground shook. Smoke rose out of the crater of Monsu Island's biggest volcano. Lava rushed down the sides.

Archie watched as Groudon stepped out from the smoke and flames. The Ground-type Pokémon was filled with power. Its whole body glowed. Groudon opened its mouth and shot a beam of light up into the clouds. The Solar Beam blasted a hole right through the storm, parting the clouds. The sun shined down on Monsu Island. Archie had never seen a Pokémon this powerful before!

He laughed in triumph.

"Groudon's here!"

# CHAPTER 16

**A**sh ran to the edge of the cliff. "There's Pikachu!" he shouted. Ash watched as his Pokémon jumped onto Groudon's forehead.

*"PI!"* Pikachu outstretched its arms in a show of power.

"What a relief!" said May.

"Pikachu is okay!" said Max.

Ash was glad to have his friends beside him. But he knew the battle was just beginning.

Kyogre swam up to meet its opponent. The two ancient Pokémon stood face-to-face. Then Groudon let out a monstrous roar.

Battle on!

Kyogre responded with a roar of its own. The sleek Pokémon dove under the water, creating another massive tidal wave.

May screamed. "This wave looks even bigger than the last one!" she shouted.

"Come on, guys!" said Max, pulling at his sister's arm. "We'd better get to higher ground—and *fast*!"

"Won't work," said Brock. "This one's so big, it'll probably swallow up the whole island." This time, Kyogre wasn't looking just to wipe out Monsu Island but *Groudon* as well.

"No!" cried Ash. "Really?!" He looked back up at Pikachu. If only he could get to his Pokémon. If only—

But there was no time. A stream of majestic light beamed down onto Groudon's head. The

ancient Pokémon threw back its head and blasted a powerful Solar Beam at the tidal wave.

Groudon's Solar Beam broke right through the tidal wave. And Pikachu was still okay.

"Groudon's *just* as powerful as Kyogre!" said Brock.

But Kyogre wasn't done yet. Both ancient Pokémon growled as they tried to figure out their opponent's next move.

"We were *fools* to believe we could actually control that kind of power," said Maxie.

"Pikachu!" Ash watched helplessly as Groudon and Pikachu stepped out into the sea. Pikachu was an Electric-type—and Electric-type Pokémon didn't work well in water. Ash had to do something. But what?

"This makes no sense!" said Lance as he circled overhead on his Dragonite. "Why would Groudon launch a Solar Beam to stop Kyogre's tsunami, unless . . . ?" Dragonite flew down and landed on the cliff ledge next to Ash.

"Ash!" Lance shouted. "Groudon is trying to stop Kyogre from destroying this island!"

"It is?!" Ash asked, confused. "It's helping us?"

"Yes," said Lance. "But in order to do that, Groudon first needed to break free. So it used the Blue Orb to ask Pikachu for *help*!"

"Oh yeah!" said Ash. Slowly, everything was beginning to make sense. "And *that's* why the Blue Orb bonded with Pikachu!" Ash looked out to where Pikachu was directing Groudon. He was proud of his Pokémon.

Pikachu raised a hand in the air. Groudon did the same. Its claws began to glow.

In one sweeping motion, Groudon slammed its fist down onto the water. A ray of light

charged across the surface and blasted Kyogre's chest. The Sea Basin Pokémon reeled backward.

"It isn't safe!" Lance called to Ash and his friends. "You've got to go while Groudon's holding off Kyogre. There's not much time!"

But Ash wasn't going anywhere without Pikachu.

"No, Lance," he said with new determination. "I'm not leaving Pikachu! You take care of the others. I'm staying here on the island!"

"But, Ash, you can't!" said Brock.

"There's no way I could run off and leave Pikachu here all alone!" Ash shouted.

He balled his hand into a fist. "I don't care what it takes. I'm gonna help! Even if I have to battle Kyogre and Groudon by myself."

"By . . . yourself?!" asked Max. He was afraid for his friend.

"Won't happen!" said Brock. He held up a Poké Ball. "'Cause I'll be right here with you!"

"Yeah, me too," said May. She clutched a Poké Ball in her fist. "We're a *team*!"

"I'll help you, too, Ash, no matter *what* blows up!" said Max.

Ash was grateful for his friends. He knew this battle wouldn't be easy, but he felt like he could do anything with Brock, May, and Max by his side.

The heroes watched as Kyogre raised itself up out of the water and shot a tunnel of water at Groudon.

"A Hydro Pump!" called Max. "That attack will be super strong against a Ground-type like Groudon!"

"Pikachu!" Ash called. He had an idea. But his Pokémon was already thinking the same thing.

*"Pika!"* Pikachu shouted as it blocked Kyogre's Hydro Pump with an electric shield.

"All right, Ash, I think you should ride with me on Dragonite," said Lance. It was time to make their move. "We'll approach Groudon and wait for the perfect opportunity to save Pikachu!"

Ash nodded.

"The rest of you guys go ahead and hop on Gyarados," Lance said to Brock, May, and Max. "See if the three of you can distract Kyogre and Archie."

"Okay, Lance!" said Brock.

Ash was so proud of his friends. He could always count on them to look out for Pikachu.

"Hey, *thanks*, you guys!" said Ash.

"Just leave it to us!" said Max.

"And please, Ash," said May, "don't do anything crazy."

"Ah, don't worry," said Ash as he climbed onto Dragonite's back. "You guys take care of yourselves, too!"

# CHAPTER 17

**A**s Lance and Ash took off, Pikachu gave Groudon a new command.

*"Pi,"* said Pikachu, and Groudon shot another Solar Beam at Kyogre. This time the ancient Water-type Pokémon was knocked back into the sea. But not for long.

Kyogre swam like a torpedo just below the surface, heading straight for Groudon. At the last moment, Kyogre dove lower and pulled the mighty Continent Pokémon down under the water.

"Oh no, *Pikachu!*" Ash cried. Electric-type Pokémon couldn't go under the water like that and stay strong!

"Stay calm, Ash," said Lance. "Just wait." Dragonite circled the spot where the two ancient Pokémon had gone under.

Ash watched as Kyogre's head resurfaced . . . followed by Groudon's. And there was Pikachu, just as tough as ever!

"*PI. KA . . .*" Pikachu clung to Groudon's head and braced itself for the next attack.

But Kyogre wasn't about to wait. It reared back, opened its flippers wide, and released a yellow beam of energy from its mouth. Groudon countered with a Mud Shot attack, blasting Kyogre's beam of light with its own shower of mud. The two beams crashed into each other and exploded.

This was May's chance. She steered Lance's red Gyarados closer to Archie.

"Beautifly, I choose you!" she called. May released her Bug-Flying-type Pokémon into the air. It flapped its shimmery blue-yellow-and-red wings.

"Now, Mudkip. Let's *go*!" shouted Brock. He threw out a Poké Ball and Mudkip leaped out, ready to use its Water-type moves.

*"MUDKIP!"* it shouted.

"Somehow, we gotta distract Archie *and* attack at the same time!" said Max.

May and Brock knew just what to do.

"Mudkip, Water Gun!" Brock called.

Mudkip spewed a cannon of water from its mouth at Archie.

"Now, Beautifly!" commanded May. "Silver Wind!"

Beautifly flapped its wings, sending curls of white light pulsing toward Archie and his hovercraft.

"What's this?!" Archie bellowed. They had his attention. "All right, Kyogre, give them what they deserve for interfering!"

"He fell for it!" Max called.

Kyogre charged the friends. Gyarados led Kyogre away from Groudon—and Pikachu.

"Kyogre's distracted!" Lance shouted as he and Ash watched from above.

Pikachu and Groudon noticed, too. Groudon fired another Solar Beam toward Kyogre. Kyogre tried to stop it with a tidal wave but wasn't fast enough. The Sea Basin Pokémon had been caught off guard. Groudon's Solar Beam hit Kyogre right in the chest, sending it flying backward into the crashing waves.

Archie screamed out as his connection to Kyogre broke. As Lance and Ash watched, the Red Orb's bond began leaving Archie's body. It was a painful separation.

Archie fainted and fell off his hovercraft toward the sea. The Red Orb floated up into the sky.

"Go!" Lance called to Dragonite. The Dragon Pokémon dove down and caught Archie in its arms just before he hit the water.

"That was a great catch, Dragonite!" Lance said.

Meanwhile, Pikachu was also crying out in pain as its connection to the Blue Orb was broken. The bond left its little yellow body, and then the Blue Orb flew up into the sky.

*"Pika! Piii-kaaaa!"* Pikachu cried.

Like Archie, Pikachu passed out as soon as the Blue Orb floated away. The tiny Pokémon wobbled and fell backward off Groudon's head.

Pikachu was plummeting toward the sea!

"Pikachu!" Ash dove into the water just as Pikachu hit the surface. The force of the fall sent Ash's buddy deep to the bottom of the ocean.

Diving down, down, down, Ash swam toward his Pokémon. He grabbed Pikachu and cradled it in his arms just before its body hit the sharp coral below.

Ash was very relieved. But they weren't safe yet.

Kyogre was swimming straight for them!

# CHAPTER 18

**B**ack on the surface, Shelly held Archie's head in her hands as he lay on the rocky shore of Monsu Island.

"Archie, sir!" she cried. "Say something! Archie!"

Archie groaned.

"Where am I . . . ?" he said, slowly opening his eyes. "Shelly! Is that you? What happened? I don't remember a thing."

"Don't worry, sir," she said. "Everything's back to normal." And it was, sort of.

At that moment, Ash and Pikachu rose up out of the sea on top of Kyogre's head.

Their friends pulled up alongside them on Gyarados's back.

"Hey, Ash! Pikachu!" Brock called. "Are you okay?"

Ash looked down at his weakened Pokémon.
A tear rolled down his cheek.

*"Pi? Pi. Ka? Pi?"* Pikachu slowly opened its eyes.

"Pikachu!" Ash shouted. He hugged his friend.

*"Pika, pi!"* Pikachu replied with a burst of energy.

"That's awesome, buddy!" said Ash. "You're okay! You're *okay!*"

Pikachu patted Kyogre's head in thanks. *"Pika pika!"*

Lance and Dragonite flew down to meet Ash. "Hop on, Ash," Lance said. Ash climbed onto Dragonite's head, and all the friends met back up on the shores of Monsu Island.

Brock was amazed at what had happened. "Thanks to Groudon, all of Kyogre's rage just vanished into thin air!" he said.

"Look up there!" said Max. He pointed toward the clouds, where the Blue and Red Orbs were doing a kind of dance in the sky. They circled around each other until they joined into one orb of bright white light. Then the light burst into tiny rays that sparkled and showered down on the friends below.

Ash and his friends watched as the two ancient Pokémon gave each other a nod, then parted ways. Groudon walked off into the smoke, and Kyogre swam deep out into the ocean. The sun began to set.

"Look," said Max. "The lava all cooled off, and now there's a lot more land!"

"And history repeats itself as once again, Groudon and Kyogre have created a new world," Lance said.

May was confused. "A new *world*?" she asked.

"Just another legend," said Lance. "The legend that Groudon and Kyogre would embody mother nature and take control over land and sea. But if humans try using the Blue and Red Orbs to *control* the two Pokémon, then they'd have no choice but to *destroy* the orbs. It's as if they were telling us that mother nature will not be controlled by selfish desire!"

"That's cool," said Ash. "I wonder if we'll ever see them again." The battle between Kyogre and Groudon had been one of the fiercest Ash had ever witnessed.

*"Pika,"* Pikachu said as it jumped up onto Ash's shoulder.

As the sun went down, Ash was left with a renewed understanding of the need for people to live peacefully with nature. And an even deeper love for his Pikachu, who had been so brave in its fight to protect the earth. He couldn't wait for their next adventure together.

**Flip over this book for another awesome Pokémon story!**